Rescued By God's Mercy

Rescued by God's Mercy

Judith Vander Wege

To Alina,

You've been a blessing to our church. I'm glad I met you.

Judy

Judith Vander Wege

Dedicated to God my Father,

who didn't give up on me when I messed up my life,

but rather showed me tender love and rescued me from my mess.

"But this is a people robbed and plundered,...trapped in holes and hidden in prisons; they have become a prey with none to rescue, a spoil with none to say, 'Restore!'" Isaiah 42:22 (RSV).

Judith Vander Wege

Endorsement:

The book of Isaiah has been a rather closed book for me, one I have never really enjoyed reading. Until I read Judy's work, I had no idea there was so much of the New Testament's Good News in this Old Testament book. Her insights dispel the notion that the God of the Old Testament was primarily a God of wrath and anger. In Isaiah, Judy finds wonderful promises of grace and forgiveness. Her openness and candor give credence to the redemptive love of God through Jesus Christ.

Tom Hydeen, Orange City, Iowa.

Rescued by Mercy

ISBN: 9781695891241

Judith Vander Wege

Printed in the United States of America.

Rescued by God's Mercy

Judith Vander Wege

Introduction

Isaiah 42:22 marks a turning point in my life, a time when I recognized the messy pit I was in and that only God could help me.

This book tells of the change that came about when I yielded my life fully to God and let him transform my life through his Word. Since then I can pray the following prayer.

Tune me up, Lord.

Bring every part of my being

into harmony with your heart and mind.

Play your beautiful music through me to express your love,

drawing others into your heart.

May I, in tune with you, speak healing to the hurting,

proclaim release to the captives, open the eyes of the blind.

Enable me always to live in harmony with your will and purpose.

Thank you, Lord, for the wonderful privilege of being your instrument.

Amen

Rescued by Mercy

In the late 1970s and early '80s, I was out of tune with my Lord and depressed. My life was not going well. It seemed our marriage was dying. I felt at the time this was my husband's fault, but I now believe there were physical, mental, emotional and spiritual reasons that I didn't realize at the time. For instance, mercury toxicity was not diagnosed until 1993, at which time I realized my symptoms had existed for twenty-three years. A mood disorder called cyclothymia also affected me. These varied yet subtle and confusing symptoms would strain any marriage.

As a result of my emotional turmoil and love hunger, I slipped into the messy pit of adultery. In chapter one, I tell more about this.

A few months later, I read the above verse from the Bible: "But *this is a people robbed and plundered,...trapped in holes and hidden in prisons; they have become a prey with none to rescue, a spoil with none to say, 'Restore!'"* Isaiah 42:22 (RSV).

"Robbed and plundered," that was me in 1982.

Gripped by Isaiah's words, I realized Satan had deceived me. He used my sense of feeling abandoned by God to trick me and I slipped into that messy pit. As I reread this verse and others in Isaiah, I began to believe that maybe God did understand me and care for me after all.

"But this is a people robbed and plundered,...trapped in holes and hidden in prisons; they have become a prey with none to rescue, a spoil with none to say, 'Restore!'" Isaiah 42:22 (RSV).

Gradually, I learned more about God's mercy as he drew me back into his heart. The book of Isaiah became instrumental in helping me change and grow. I became more intimate with Almighty God who forgave me, rescued me, and restored me to a relationship with himself.

Meanwhile, I learned about others who were also deceived and living in "the pits." The desire grew to share with them that God can restore us to spiritual and emotional health, to intimacy with Himself through his mercy and grace. I hope this book will help my readers to embrace God's mercy in a deeper way, leading to a wholehearted trust in God.

"Mercy is when God forgives us, rescues us from the messes we've made, and lovingly restores us to relationship with himself."

"Grace is when he gives us the undeserved gift of relationship with himself."

Out of Tune and Into the Pit

My heart thumped as the door opened. *This time he had been gone for a week. How would he react to my letter? Was I wrong to write it?*

My husband joined me in the kitchen with no "hello" or kiss in greeting. He just dropped a question in mid-air: "I'm thinking we should move to Canada. Do you want to go to Canada with me?"

Panic stuck in my throat. *Why would he want to leave a good job and go to Canada where we had no connections? Was he planning to move us all to Canada and then divorce me? What would I do then, abandoned where nobody knew us?*

Fear erased the last doubt about the letter I had agonized over.

I answered his question, "No," and handed him my letter. It began with the firm statement: "These are the reasons we need to get a divorce."

I fought tears and ran down the stairs, pretending I had to work in the laundry room. He followed with the letter and sat on the lowest step to read it. I watched his face, hoping I was mistaken.

Judith Vander Wege

For five years I had prayed God would heal my husband's depression and our marriage. *Certainly it must be God's will to heal our marriage, isn't it?* But I saw no answer to my prayer.

We had both been Christians most of our lives. We believed "Divorce was not an option."

*****

My spiritual journey began early. My parents had me baptized as a baby in 1943. At age six, my Sunday School teacher looked directly at me and said with a smile, "Jesus loves you."

But the most momentous encounter came when I was nine years old. After an evangelistic meeting, I heard Jesus whisper into my right ear, "I want to be personal to you, too. Do you say yes or no?"

I said "yes" to Jesus and it seemed as if a light turned on in my soul. Thereafter, I loved going to church, Sunday School, Luther League, reading the Bible and attending Bible Camp throughout my teenage years.

After graduating from nurses' training, I married and was fairl happy for twelve years. Then my world began to fall apart. We had tw beautiful adopted children, aged six and eight, when our youngest was born. It had taken me eleven years to become pregnant, and we were all thrilled. However, I had trouble recovering from the difficult delivery. My neck and back muscles hurt and I felt generally unwell and tired. My only joy was cuddling my precious baby. At the time we did not know I had mercury toxicity and cyclothymia. A year or so later, I wrote this poem showing how I felt:

The Greater Gift

"Lord, give me clear sailing," is what I often cry
when I feel the fog's so thick I'd really rather die.
Then, just for a moment, he'll cause the fog to lift.
And he says, "My grace, sufficient, is the greater gift.
"When at last, you've stood the test," he gently lets me know,
"you'll receive the crown of life. The trials help you grow."

As time went on, someone said potassium deficiency could cause depression. So I started taking a potassium supplement and began to feel a little better. Meanwhile, my husband's depression grew worse. I kept praying about his depression and tried to help him, but he seemed to push me away. He stayed at the office more and more.

By the fourth year of this, I was convinced my husband's depression was due to the fact he felt trapped in a marriage to me. *He must want out of the marriage,* I thought. My heart was broken by rejection.

One day, as I played the piano, it seemed Jesus sang "Comfort" to my heart. He directed me toward prayer as a way to joy, pledged me his friendship and faithfulness, reminded me he came to set me free. H asked me to give my heart to him and promised to give me abundant li when I learned to trust him.

Comfort

"Let me sing a song to you. Let me know if you are feeling blue.

Wipe those tears away. Lift your eyes and pray.

"I will be your friend, love you till the end.

For I came to save you from the tyranny of sin.

"Give your life to me. Life abundantly

is what I will give you

when you trust in me to set you free."

I will wipe away your tears. Perfect love will cast out all your fears.

Yes, I gave my life, just to end your strife.

When you come to me, gold is what I see.

I know you are precious and I want you to be mine.

Clouded now by sin, dirt and dross within.

Yield to my refining.

When the trials are done, how you will shine.

© 1980--"Comfort" by Judith Vander Wege

I should have clung to the comfort of this song. But by the fifth year of my husband's depression, I was out of tune with God. When God did not answer my prayers the way I wanted, I quit trusting him to work for good in my life. I still believed Jesus died for me and I would live eternally, *but where was the abundant life he promised in John 10:10?*

I felt God did not care about my happiness in this life,--that he had abandoned me. In my grief, I became angry at God. Instead of trusting him, I began to believe a sneering voice that seemed to whisper: "God doesn't care about your life here. He just wants numbers in heaven. That's why he 'saved' you. Grab happiness where you can."

These lies began to make more sense than the Bible as my hope faded and my trust in God dimmed. Then Satan conveniently provided someone to lead me astray.

A fellow who was supposedly trying to recover from drug addiction and alcoholism joined our Old Time Fiddlers Group. He asked me questions about Christianity. I tried to answer them, wanting to help him become a Christian. A few months earlier, I had asked God for opportunities to witness to people. So when he asked about Christianity, I thought he was an assignment from God.

Before long, he told me I was beautiful. In my state of despair, I was hungry to hear those words. Letting my feelings rule more than the Holy Spirit and starved for love and admiration, I fell for his manipulations and flattery. I proceeded down that dark path and slippe into the slimy pit of adultery. At first, I did not recognize it as rebellio or idolatry. I did not intend to reject God's plan. Rather, I fell for the deception of thinking this path *was* obedience. After all, I was trying to show Christ-like love to this man.

Besides, I thought, *it would set my unhappy husband free. Wasn't that the loving thing to do?*

It was the day before our 17th wedding anniversary when I gave my husband the letter stating we needed to divorce. I watched his face and saw only relief. That confirmed my suspicions. He did not need me or want me in his life. He immediately organized a "trusting divorce" with his name as the petitioner.

Through adultery and divorce, I lost my home, financial security, children, ministry at church, reputation, self-respect, and my peace of mind. Rebellion and idolatry are costly.

Six and a half months later, believing my addict boyfriend was recovering and in love with me, I married him. I soon discovered he was not abstaining from marijuana or alcohol as I had thought. During the next three years, my life worsened with the stress, insecurity, poverty and frustration of living with a practicing addict. My life was miserable, and eventually, dangerous. I was "robbed and plundered… trapped in holes...with no one to rescue" ---deceived, cheated and trapped by Satan.

Judith Vander Wege

It felt like I was in a pit of quicksand. According to *HowStuffWorks.com*, the best way to get out of quicksand is to quit struggling. I was definitely struggling—not only to do what I thought was right, but also to get my new husband to do what was right. Searching for answers, I attended Al-Anon. This experience taught me that I could not solve anyone else's problems, but I could get help for my own.

Al-Anon helped me emotionally, but my biggest agony was spiritual. *How could I have fallen into this pit? How could I, a "good girl," have failed so totally to be a good witness for Christ? Did I forever destroy God's plan for my life? Why did God let this happen?* I was full of questions and confusion about how to think.

As I prayed, my feelings began to form into a poem. The "Pray of Confusion," helped me even as I wrote it. When I asked the Lord Jesus to take control of my life, the answers I needed came into focus.

Prayer of Confusion

Will somebody tell me how to live?

What is the secret? How do I give?

How do I yield my heart?

Rescued by Mercy

Will somebody tell me who I am?

Which is the truth and which but a sham?

How did deception start?

What are the answers?

I need them now

to questions I can't figure out somehow.

Am I wise or am I a fool?

Am I loving or am I cruel?

How do I listen and who will speak?

I feel confused and amazingly weak.

O Lord, take control of my inner soul.

Where I am lacking, please make me whole.

Search me and make me true.

For you are the one who gave me life!

Tell me the secret, thus end my strife.

Teach me to live for you!

After a few months, I found a church that accepted us. By

this time I felt terribly guilty for my adultery. Marrying him had not resolved that guilt. I also still suffered the grief of divorce, which felt like a tragic train wreck hurting everyone in our family. Feeling I had failed God, I sought his forgiveness.

This church (appropriately named Hope) helped me heal spiritually. It seemed God spoke directly to my heart when they prayed Scripture over me with their hands on my head, for instance: "*I have loved you with an everlasting love [says the Lord]; therefore I have continued my faithfulness to you. Again I will build you and you shall be built"* (Jeremiah 31:3-4 RSV).

One of the members of my new church decided to be my "big sister." She knew something of my struggles and recommended I go to a Basic Youth Conflicts Seminar. While there I heard words to this effect: "When your heart breaks at the things that break God's hea that's true repentance."

The talks showed me my hidden attitudes. Besides the adultery I was guilty of resentment, bitterness, selfishness, pride, and idolatry. I had always thought of myself as basically obedient to parents and to God. But at this time I noticed my rebellion.

As I thought of God's heart breaking over these sinful attitudes, my heart broke. I repented fully. More than anything else, I wanted a restored relationship with my Lord and Heavenly Father. God loved me in spite of my sin and he was calling me back to himself. I was astounded at God's mercy.

After returning home, I called my parents and asked them to forgive me for bad attitudes. They seemed surprised, but assured me, "If there's anything to forgive, of course we forgive you."

They had not known the attitudes in my heart and mind. But I knew and God knew. Calling them gave me a degree of peace of mind and improved our relationship.

Like one dying of thirst, I began to soak up scriptures. The book of Isaiah, especially, gave me hope. Isaiah 42:22 soon gripped my heart, for I felt like one "robbed and plundered" and trapped. The entire book of Isaiah showed me a merciful God who longed to rescue. I grew to love Isaiah's book.

Isaiah is called the evangelical prophet because he spoke good news. God's mercy certainly was good news to me. As I read, I began to know the heart of God more clearly. He is not an angry God desiring to punish, but rather a loving Father, weeping over the estrangement of his children. He agonizes over the consequences his children must suffer as a result of their disobedience.

Isaiah's inspired words helped me repent and grow into a deeper intimacy with God who forgave me and rescued me from the "pit" of sin. I became convinced God longs to restore us all to fellowship with himself, to spiritual and emotional health.

Prayer:

Dear Father, keep me in tune with you. You promised no one will snatch me out of your hand, but Satan is so sneaky. Don't let him pull me away from your heart. Hold me close to your heart, Lord. Let your wisdom always guide my mind that I will know what to do in every situation. My heart's desire is to do your will—to never fail you again, never disappoint you again, never give a disgraceful slur to your name again. In Jesus' Name, Amen.

Rebellion Versus Mercy

Rebellion led me into my "pit." When I repented, God began to lift me out of it. Let's look at what Isaiah says about rebellion:

For the LORD speaks: 'I raised children, I brought them up, but they have rebelled against me! An ox recognizes its owner, a donkey recognizes where its owner puts its food; but Israel does not recognize me, my people do not understand'" (Isaiah 1:2–3 NET).

As I reread chapter one of Isaiah, I sensed the heart of God, broken by his rebellious children. These children are not toddlers who keep falling down because they cannot help it. He has raised them. They should know better, because the most loving father in the whole universe has taught them for many years. They should know by now they can trust him. Because they don't trust God, they rebel and go their own way.

Isaiah's words are those of a man who lives intimately with the Lord God Almighty, the "Holy One of Israel." Isaiah knows how God feels. He tries to reason with the people who have rebelled.

I should have known better, too, for I had been God's child for nearly three decades. This verse spoke to me: "*Why should you be beaten anymore? Why do you persist in rebellion? Your whole head is injured, your whole heart afflicted,*" (Isaiah 1:5 NIV).

My present problems were consequences of my own disobedience. Like Eve in the Garden of Eden, I was injured, afflicted and desolate because of my rebellion.

In order to show how harmful rebellion is and why it is sometimes necessary for a parent to allow the rebel to suffer, I wrote a fiction story called The Runaway. This story shows how I think God feels about his rebellious children. It can be found for sale at https://judithvanderwege (my website product page), and at Amazon.com.

Isaiah, the evangelical prophet, revealed the heart of God broken over his rebellious people. He tried to reason with them to turn to the Lord: "*Come now, let us reason together,*" says the Lord. "*Though your sins are like scarlet, they shall be white as snow. Thoug they are red as crimson, they shall be as wool. If you are willing and obedient, you will eat the best of the land*" (Isaiah 1:18-19, NIV). This sounds like the Lord loves to forgive. He longs for his rebellious children to return to him so he can bless them.

Isaiah tells of his encounter with God at the beginning of his ministry. He saw God as high and lifted up and "his train filled the temple." Isaiah said, "Woe is me for I am lost," because he knew he was sinful, (Isaiah 6:5-7).

We also need to be cleansed by Jesus, who died for us, before we can fit into God's plan for our lives. Isaiah had a purpose in God's plan, but first he needed to be cleansed. Just as the burning coal did not destroy Isaiah's lips but rather cleansed them, God's judgment is never meant to destroy. God wants to bring people into right relationship with him. God wants pure vessels he can use.

I began to understand why I had to go through tough times. I needed to see my sin for what it was before I could be forgiven. Then I could rejoice in my cleansing.

God transformed Isaiah's life with a vision of himself. He gave me a vision, too. During a painful and scary incident, he enabled me to trust him better.

Judith Vander Wege

One night, my second husband came home at 2 am stoned and drunk. He woke me up and insisted I go to the store and get him some cigarettes. Although I had previously acted like a submissive wife, Al-Anon taught me to quit being an enabler. I asked God to guide me and help me. Since I did not approve of smoking, should I help my husband do something that was bad for his health? Besides, it was a ridiculous request at two in the morning.

So I meekly said, "No."

He acted like he didn't believe me. "I jus' need some cig'rettes and my truck's out o' gas. You take your car and go get me some."

"No" I said again, firmly.

He "explained" again, then clenched both hands around my neck. When I still refused, he squeezed tighter. It really hurt, but I managed to get a finger under his hands so I could breathe and talk. "If you kill me, I'll go to heaven, but you'll have it on your conscience for the rest of your life." Then I silently prayed.

After a few moments, he rolled over into a drunken stupor. As I lay there in the midst of heartaches and fears, with my neck aching, I cried out to Jesus, "Do you want me to hurt like this?"

With the eyes of my heart, I saw Jesus nearby weeping as if his heart would break. He shook his head and said, “No! No, I don't want you to hurt like that. I love you!”

Confused, I wondered why he didn't take me out of my situation. But I believed him. *He loves me! He doesn’t want me to hurt.* Then the thought occurred, *He looks like he’s waiting for me to do something. What is it?*

Trembling, I got up quietly, hoping my husband would not awaken. I called a friend who was a social worker and told him what had happened. He agreed to come stay at our house the rest of the night, to make sure I was safe. I moved to the guest room and tried to sleep.

In the morning, the social worker tried to talk sense to my husband. I called our pastor and he sent a Christian couple over to counsel with us. When my husband saw the marks on my neck, he agreed to weekly counseling and to abstaining from alcohol and marijuana. He seemed sober for the next six weeks, so I thought maybe the choking incident was turning into some good. He had never been sober that long since I met him.

My vision of seeing Jesus weeping over me gave me comfort. Believing he loved me gave me the courage to trust him completely. I asked Jesus to take back the throne of my heart, and I determined to obey him. I needed to leave idolatry behind. My heart and mind needed to change from rebellion against God to submission and obedience to him.

I kept praying my second husband's heart and life would change, too, but I saw no change in him. (The choking incident happened two years after we married. During that time, I lived with confusion. How should I deal with my husband's lack of trustworthiness, his alcoholic behavior, and his lack of contributing to the family finances? Al-Anon said, "Don't enable your spouse's addictions," yet I was trying to show him Christ-like love. How could I do that without enabling?

This marriage did not improve either. After six weeks, my husband was back to his partying lifestyle. A few weeks after the choking incident and during the weekly counseling, I found out he was smoking marijuana daily. Since he was not staying sober as he promised, I felt a sense of impending doom.

The church offered to pay for him to go to Teen Challenge, which helps people recover from alcoholism and addictions. He refused. Problems escalated until I needed to choose either to stay on a conveyor belt to destruction or divorce him.

My pastor said, “We can’t change him, but we can help you.”

So the church paid for me to get counseling. At the third session with a Christian psychiatrist, after he heard of the latest incident, he said, “Let’s pray.”

After praying together, the psychiatrist said, “I saw a vision of him coming after you with a knife and I was standing between. Pray more about this and talk to your pastor before you decide for sure, but I think you should separate.”

I called my pastor to tell him the recommendation. He and an elder changed the locks on my mobile home and took my husband’s belongings to his temporary job.

He called me a few times, trying to manipulate me into letting him back in. But I felt I just could not handle it anymore. He already had seven “dramatic turnarounds” in the three years we had been together. I now knew I could not save him,

Judith Vander Wege

After our divorce, he did say one sweet thing that made me feel better: "God sent me an angel to show me the way, but I wouldn't listen to her."

Immanuel

"I will come to you and fulfill my gracious promise to bring you back...For I know the plans I have for you,' declares the Lord, 'plans to prosper you and not to harm you, plans to give you hope and a future" (Jeremiah 29:11 NIV). Thus Scripture continued to reinforce God's message of love.

Another verse, meaningful since childhood, stood out for me: *"And we know that in all things God works for the good of those who love him, who have been called according to his purpose,"* (Romans 8:28 NIV).

God does not force us to fit into his good plans. He lets us choose whether to follow him or not. Moses said, "*I have set before you life and death, blessing and curse; therefore choose life, that you and your descendants may live, loving the Lord your God, obeying his voice, and cleaving to him; for that means life to you and length of days that you may dwell in the land,*" (Deuteronomy 30:19–20 RSV).

When turmoil came into my life, I had failed to obey God. Although I had been a Christian for almost 30 years, I lacked trust in him. The consequences of my disobedience brought me more suffering, but God reached out to me with his mercy and healed me with his love. This special relationship with Almighty God was the abundant life I had been looking for. God astounded me with his mercy. As I learned to trust the Lord better and let him have control of my life, peace replaced much of the inner turmoil.

Several times in the Bible, we are encouraged to ask God for a sign that he will do what he promised: Zechariah 10:1 RSV, "*Ask the Lord for rain in the springtime.*"

Matthew 7:7-9 RSV, "*Ask and it will be given to you; seek and you will find; knock and the door will be opened to you.*"

John 16:24b, "*Ask and you will receive, and your joy will be complete.*

Isaiah knew that somehow, sometime, God would carry out a plan of salvation that would change people's hearts and lives from rebellion to joyful submission and obedience. Meanwhile, he encouraged the people who already believed by telling them "*God is with us*." We can still trust Immanuel.

Those who believe in God, trusting and obeying him, have

the security and joy of his presence. Current events in the world often cause fear and anxiety. Hopefully, we can learn from the messages of Scripture. As long as we walk with God in trust and obedience, God will protect us and gave us peace.

Notice the following verse: "*They sought God eagerly and he was found by them. So the Lord gave them rest on every side*" (Second Chronicles.15:15b NIV),

If we "fear" the Lord, (revere him *and* trust in him), we need fear nothing else. The only time to be afraid is when we go outside of God's will.

The Prince of Peace, also called Messiah, was God Almighty, come to earth in the person of Jesus Christ in order to reconcile humankind with himself.

"God was in Christ reconciling the world to himself, not counting their trespasses against them, and entrusting to us the ministry of reconciliation."

To reconcile means to take away the enmity between humans and God, to remove the offense. Jesus came to earth to be Immanuel (God with us). After he arose from the dead and returned to Heaven, he sent his Holy Spirit to be with us in the midst of our trials and tribulations of daily life.

Jesus will come again someday in glory and power, victorious over our enemies: sin, death, and the devil. We who are his people will thereafter live in perfect joy and peace with him without any more sin, trials, or tribulations. If we are centered in him, (if we put our trust in Jesus Christ and follow him obediently), we have no need to fear.

Those who believe in God, trusting and obeying him, have the security and joy of his presence. Current events in the world often cause fear and anxiety. But hopefully, we can learn from the messages of Scripture. As long as we walk with God in trust and obedience, God will protect us and gave us peace.

Jesus will come again someday in glory and power, victorious over our enemies: sin, death, and the devil. We who are his people will thereafter live in perfect joy and peace with him without any more sin trials, or tribulations. If we are centered in him, (if we put our trust in Jesus Christ and follow him obediently), we have no need to fear.

Rescued by Mercy

Prayer: *Thank you, God, that you are merciful even while you are disciplining us. Thank you for teaching us, for bringing us to repentance so we can experience your forgiveness and cleansing. Thanks for using our trials to refine and purify us. Enable us to bear fruit for your kingdom. Amen*

God Makes Himself Known

"But there will be no gloom for her that was in anguish...the people who walked in darkness have seen a great light; those who dwelt in a land of deep darkness, on them has light shined." (Isaiah 9:1a,2 RSV)

The above verses lightened my heart. I was done walking in darkness! I remembered when, as a child, the light had been turned on in my soul after Jesus told me he wanted to be personal to me. The light had dimmed for a time as an adult, but now it shone brightly agai

God is the light. If a person shuts out God from his or her life, i is like going into a dark cellar and shutting the door. The person will stumble around in the darkness.

When I refused to believe in God's great love, the light had dimmed for me. I looked at my circumstances and doubted God cared about my happiness. I thought he had abandoned me. Looking at circumstances alone can drag us into the darkness of depression and despair. Yet, God does care about our happiness.

These scriptures from the NIV underscore this truth:

"*Cast all your anxiety on him because he cares for you,*" (First Peter 5:7).

Rescued by Mercy

"Delight yourself in the Lord and he will give you the desires of your heart," (Psalm 37:4).

"You have made known to me the path of life; you will fill me with joy in your presence, with eternal pleasures at your right hand," (Psalm 16:11).

"But God demonstrates his love for us in this: while we were still sinners, Christ died for us," (Rom. 5:8.)

Verses like these and many others were like a healing balm to me. I was astounded at the mercy of God conveyed in Isaiah and other places in the Bible. I didn't deserve mercy, yet he offered it. Discipline comes for us if we rebel against the Lord who created us and redeemed us in love. But even the discipline of the Almighty holy God is merciful. His purpose is to teach us the right way to live in a right relationship with him.

Have you ever caught your child doing something dangerous? What do you do? If your three year-old runs into a busy street to get a ball or your teenager uses drugs, how do you react?

God is love. Yet, his discipline is necessary. Loving parents ought to get angry when their children put themselves in danger by refusing to follow the rules. If they do not get angry, it is a sign of indifference.

We try to teach our children to obey because we love them. We want them to be safe. Sometimes they think we are mean, but in spite o their reactions, we discipline them. Likewise The Lord disciplines thos he loves.

Isaiah predicted Immanuel, the Messiah God would send, woul bring us freedom from the oppression of our enemy, Satan. After feeli trapped in my guilt and shame, and bearing the consequences of my si this was wonderful news for me.

When God disciplined me, I was relieved that the discipline—although painful—was not as severe as I had feared. It reassured me o God's involvement in my life. He had not abandoned me. Rather, his discipline helped me repent and trust God. Since he kept his promise t discipline me, I believed he would also keep his promises to bless me. This was good news.

For me, here and now, Immanuel means I'm never alone. Whe

I need comfort, wisdom, advice, direction, inspiration, companionship, or even conviction, God is present. Jesus was and is Immanuel. After he rose from the dead and returned to heaven, he sent his Holy Spirit to be Immanuel (God with us). He is with us today.

Prayer: *Thank you, holy, all-powerful God for loving us. What an awesome truth that you would call us into fellowship with yourself in order to shower your blessings on us! Thank you that your light has dawned so we can know you intimately, even as your adopted children. May we all experience your light, so we can get to know you and the power of your resurrection.*

We pray for all who read these pages that your light will dawn in their hearts also, so they can know you and the power of your resurrection. *In Jesus' name, Amen.*

Judith Vander Wege

The Branch

"There shall come forth a shoot from the stump of Jesse, and a branch shall grow out of his roots. And the Spirit of the LORD shall rest upon him, the spirit of wisdom and understanding, the spirit of counsel and might, the spirit of knowledge and the fear of the Lord."

(Isaiah 11:1-2 RSV).

In Isaiah's time and later, most of the royal line of David did not follow God. Neither did the nation. Therefore, Isaiah prophesied judgment. The royal line of David would be cut off, chopped down like a tree. The people must have wondered about Isaiah's prophecy. How could the Messiah come from the line of David if it was cut off? Yet, because of forgiveness, Messiah would rule a remnant.

The Messiah King will rule in righteousness, equity, wisdom and faithfulness. His kingdom will be peaceful. Both people and animals will live with each other in love and security.

Christians have a small glimpse already of what this new kingdom will be like. As we grow in Christ, we become more loving and begin to exhibit the fruit of the Spirit which is love, joy, peace, patience, kindness, goodness, gentleness, faithfulness, and self-control.

Although already justified before God because of faith in Jesus, we still have sinful natures and slip into sin. We struggle against temptations. But in heaven, there will be no sin. We will not have to fight the temptations of our old natures but will be able to live the way God desires.

After Israel fell into idolatry, it was cut off in judgment. Isaiah's picture of Israel as a tree which God cut down (11:1-5), is sobering. I often wonder—will he cut down America? Many people seem to ignore God or rebel against him. Idolatry is rampant in materialism and other self-centered lifestyles as well as other cultural 'idols'. I experienced something like this when I obeyed the 'idol' of my emotions rather than God's Word.

Judgment may come in individual lives as natural consequences of our sins, or our nation may be conquered by some other regime. But praise God for his mercy! He does not leave nations or individuals stuck in our messes. He rescues and redeems those who are willing. I discovered this truth after my life was cut down. Slowly and surely, a shoot rose from the stump. Jesus became the "Branch" to me in a new way. I realized how vital he is to my life. I needed to cling to him in trust and obedience. It was a matter of life or death. He taught me how to keep my covenant, to *delight* in God (Psalm 37:4 and 1:2).

The Apostle Paul describes Jesus when he writes, "*For in him all the fullness of God was pleased to dwell, and through him to reconcile to himself all things, whether on earth or in heaven, making peace by the blood of his cross.*(Colossians1:19–20 and 2:9 RSV).

Jesus preached good news to the poor, set the captives free, healed the blind, helped the oppressed, suffered and died for our salvation, brought judgment and eternal life to us.

Remember God's first promise to Adam and Eve that the seed of the woman would step on the head of the serpent?(Gen. 3:15). By his death and resurrection, Jesus "trampled on the head" of Satan, conquering that devil and rescuing enslaved souls.

From the perspective of believers, Jesus has already won. But he has not yet completely eradicated evil in our world. After his final defeat of evil, Jesus Christ will usher in the Kingdom of God describe in Isaiah11:6–16. He will stand as an ensign (a banner) and people from all over will come to him. What a glorious day that will be when Christ is lifted up to draw all eyes and hearts to himself.

Since Jesus provided the way, all we need to do is admit we are sinners in need of salvation, believe that Jesus—the Son of God—died to save us, believe he rose again, and receive him as our Savior and Lord.

The commentator Matthew Henry explains, "Everything that might hinder the progress and success of the Gospel shall be taken out of the way." In other words, when God's time comes "for the bringing of nations, or particular persons, home to himself, divine grace will be victorious over all opposition" (M.H.1102).

Whether this victory comes in our present lives or in the great ending battle of Armageddon, believers will naturally break out in praise when we realize he is our salvation.

A personal relationship with God is what makes it possible for us to draw close to Jesus. The Holy Spirit helps us in our journey.

Christians are already rescued and set free from slavery to the evil one. Yet evil is still rampant on the earth and often affects us. We are not yet living in the Messianic Kingdom described in Isaiah 11:6–10. We are enlisted to engage in a holy war against Satan. (Note that our "holy war" is not against people, but against the spiritual force of darkness, (see Ephesians 6:12)).

Jesus died and rose again to set us free from Satan. When we follow Jesus, we are called to die to self. He gives the example of a grain of wheat. When it is planted, it dies and bears fruit (see John 12:24–26 and Galatians 2:20). Dying to self means letting Jesus be on the throne of our hearts.

Becoming a Christian is like joining an army. Satan does not need to attack those who are still under his command. But when we leave Satan's army, we become his enemies. Therefore, he attacks us with a vengeance. It is not a worldly war, but a spiritual one.

In his mercy, God provides the spiritual armor and weapons we need. These are listed in Ephesians 6:10–18. According to the Apostle Paul in Romans 8:31–39, there is no chance of Satan defeatin us if we are "in Christ Jesus," fighting this war on God's side.

Isaiah leads us to look at God's messages as if looking at a mountain range from the top of a peak. We can see the next closest one, but we can also see nearby mountains. At the same time, we can see one farther off and others in the distance. The entire Bible is God's message to us. It all ties together with the main message being salvation. One part explains another.

I became overwhelmed by God's mercy and convinced God cared about me. He wanted me to experience life abundantly. Even his judgment was merciful as it warned me gently to turn from my sin, thereby protecting me from personal destruction.

If we accept his mercy, he works in our lives for good. He considers us valuable enough to teach us to trust. He also reveals Father God to us, dwells among us and gives us grace.

Prayer:

Thank you, Lord, that you don't leave nations or individuals in the messes we get ourselves into. Mercifully, you rescue us. We praise you for providing the spiritual armor and weapons we need to fight the battle against Satan and his forces.

In your name, Lord Jesus, I put on the belt of truth, for you are the way, the truth and the life. In you all things hold together. I accept your righteousness as my breastplate, and I put on the shoes that enable me to walk in peace. In your name I put on the helmet of salvation, for "I know whom I have believed, and am convinced that he is able to guard what I have entrusted to him for that day"(Second Timothy 1:12).

Thank you for the shield of faith—you are a shield about me—and for the sword of the Spirit which is the Word of God. I will use it to fight like Jesus did. In Jesus' name, Amen

Red Thread of Redemption

If you heard someone say, "Someone is coming!" would you respond with joy, excitement, or fear? It would depend, wouldn't it? As my personal Bible Study continued, I was impressed with how it all tied together. I'd heard of a "red thread of redemption" connecting the entire Bible. Now I paid more attention and found it meaningful.

Adam and Eve were afraid because they knew they had sinned. So they hid in the garden. Of course they could not hide from God for long, and when he found them he pronounced the consequences of their disobedience.

This was serious. God had given them the responsibility for caring for the Garden, to be masters of all life upon the earth. But by their disobedience, it was as if they handed over their responsibilities to Satan. Now Satan, the evil one, would be prince of the earth.

Yet God desired to redeem Adam and Eve, (redeem means to buy back); so he gave his first promise—the first part of a red thread of redemption that stretches throughout the Bible. God said someone would come from the seed of the woman who would defeat the evil

Judith Vander Wege

one (Genesis 3:15 NIV). This someone would be the Messiah.

The Bible reveals, little by little, God's plan to restore people to fellowship with himself through this anointed one. Isaiah calls him a "branch" and a "shoot from the stump of Jesse,”

From the line of Adam and Eve's third son, Seth, Noah was bor Noah was a type of Christ," in that he was the “only truly righteous ma living on the earth at that time, (Genesis 6:10 LAB)

About ten generations after Noah, Abram was born. God calle him to be the Father of his chosen nation, then asked him to sacrifice his son. Abraham was commended for this difficult obedience after G stopped the sacrifice.

Joseph, the son of Jacob, was a type of Christ in that he was unjustly sold into slavery, and unjustly accused, but eventually saved his people from starvation. He forgave his brothers just as Jesus Chris later forgave his murderers. God's purpose in choosing the nation of Israel was to bring his plan of salvation to people all over the world.

Four hundred years after Joseph, God chose Moses to rescue his people out of slavery. The Passover lamb before the Exodus is a foreshadow of Jesus, our Paschal lamb who died in our place to rescue us out of the slavery of sin. According to Galatians 4:3-7, the reason Jesus rescued us was so he could adopt us as his children.

God called King David a man after his own heart. Even though he sinned, he sincerely repented. The usual attitude of his heart was love for God and obedience to him. God promised one of David's descendants would reign over God's kingdom forever. That prophecy was fulfilled in Jesus. The king of peace would come from the line of David, bringing in a righteous kingdom. The Spirit of the Lord would rest on this king, Jesus.

Promises continue throughout scripture. They help us understand better the salvation God planned.

At the end of our age, the world system will make war against Jesus. "*But the Lamb will overcome them because he is Lord of lords and King of kings,*" Revelation 17:14 NIV).

This promise shown in Revelation completes the Red Thread of Redemption. The world system will fall, and Jesus will reign forever. Then we who belong to him will be with him in heaven. Hallelujah!

Judith Vander Wege

Prayer:

Thank you Father for your wonderful plan of salvation. Thank you for sending your Messiah, Jesus Christ, to reconcile us to yourself. In Jesus name, Amen.

;.\

Merciful Judgment

"You will say in that day: 'I will give thanks to thee, O LORD,
for though thou wast angry with me, thy anger turned away and thou didst comfort me.
Behold, God is my salvation; I will trust, and will not be afraid;
for the LORD God is my strength and my song, and he has become my salvation.'"
(Isaiah 12:1–6, RSV)

Isaiah 12 is highlighted bright red in my Bible with the note, "This is true for me now!" 4-12-97. By that time, I was healthier, emotionally and spiritually. I was also in a different, more loving and stable marriage.

Physically I was much improved, also, after the Lord led me to a doctor skilled at finding the root of chronic illnesses. He diagnosed my mercury toxicity and treated it. He told me to have my dental fillings replaced with composite fillings. After that was done in 1995, I began a gradual climb to health. The emotional condition of cyclothymia had not yet been diagnosed, so I still had trouble with moods, handling stress and other problems. But in comparison to the previous twenty years, I felt much better. Therefore. I sincerely prayed the hymn in Isaiah 12 and can do so even more today. I praise God the powers of darkness did not destroy me. God's forgiveness and comfort became my strength, song and salvation. Now I can "draw water from the wells of salvation" (verse 3). Out of gratitude, I want to "make known among the nations what he has done," (verse 4), to write, proclaim and sing about my glorious Lord.

However, the next few chapters of Isaiah (chapters 13-23) remained black and white in my Bible. I did not like to read about prophecies of judgment for myself or anyone else. I wanted mercy. Yet I searched deeper. How could I get any use out of this passage? In more concentrated study, I found valuable truths in these chapters. The first truth is not a new one but stressed in a poignant way: God is against wickedness. *No duh*! *Of course he is*!

But let's think of the deeper implication. He is not only against the wickedness around us, but also against the sin within us. Often, the troubles God allows us to go through help to purify us.

The second truth apparent in these chapters is that God does not enjoy punishing people, even if they are wicked. His desire is to bring people to repentance.

We have often failed to trust God and need tutoring. Yet we can be convinced and comforted by the truth that God's purpose in judging and disciplining us is to rescue us from Satan's traps — to draw us into his heart. God hates sinful pride. We depend for our very existence on the continued grace of a loving Creator. Therefore, how can we act as if we are somehow "King of the Hill?

I had never thought of myself as a prideful or rebellious person, but this truth convicted me. When I became angry at God for not answering my prayers the way I wanted, wasn't I in essence telling him I knew better than he how to run my life? Later, when he showed me the condition of my heart, I saw the attitudes of self-righteousness, bitterness, and pride. That broke my heart. His merciful judgment brought me to repentance.

Humans could not exist were it not for Almighty God. How can we lift ourselves up in arrogance against the very one who gives us breath?

Judith Vander Wege

God is trustworthy because God is love. He is also powerful enough to do what is right for us. Because of the sinfulness of humankind, it is right that judgment comes before mercy. We need to know and admit our sinfulness before we can receive forgiveness.

When I returned to the Lord and received forgiveness, I gained the confidence I needed to live a Christian life. Trusting God brought grace sufficient for whatever task he called me to do.

In the universal picture, our compassionate God wars against wickedness. Satan is the one who has enslaved and oppressed all humankind. To the contrary, God desires to set us all free. God hates evil and will eventually eradicate it . God's agent to set humankind free is his Son, Jesus Christ, who defeated Satan at the cross.

Even God's judgment is merciful. Its purpose is to set free those who will accept his love. God judges in order to drive us to Christ, who can free us from our sin and reconcile us to God. The first and most important of the Ten Commandments says, "Worship no other god but me" (Exodus 20:3 TLB). God does not need praise. He is not an egomaniac. But he knows we become like what we worship.

If we worship the Most High God who is holy, merciful,

loving and forgiving, we will become like him. If we worship money, we become greedy and selfish. If we worship another person to the point that we do what that person wants rather than what God wants, that is also idolatry.

A god is something or someone that has a hold on one's life. When we worship Almighty God as revealed in Jesus Christ, we are giving him our allegiance, letting him have control of our lives. If we let something or someone else have first place in our lives, we are in essence rejecting the real God. It is a matter of a person's heart allegiance. God wants a personal relationship with us for our good. As our Creator, he knows if we put anything other than him at the center of our lives, we will not reach the potential he created in us.

God does not enjoy judging or disciplining people. It hurts him to see those he loves hurting. Yet he knows what is necessary in order to bring them to repentance. I'm glad God called me to repentance rather than giving up on me.

Prayer: *Dear Jesus, you are my Lord, and you are my King. You alone have the right to rule from the throne of my heart. Help me to be a faithful subject and do all you have assigned for me to do. Amen*

Judith Vander Wege

God Can Use Evil For Good

God is merciful. His judgment is never meant to destroy, but to bring people into right relationships with him--- to purify us. God wants pure vessels he can use. We will be happiest if we learn to trust him and fit into his wonderful plans.

People often think of trials and tragedies as punishments. Think of what Joseph went through in Genesis 37-50. After his brothers sold him into slavery, he was taken to Egypt, and put in jail for something he did not do. But God worked in his life and through him. Several years later, his brothers came to Egypt to buy food and Joseph gave it to them. He forgave them. God had used all his trials for good to keep many from starving during the famine.

The story of Job is another example of how God works in everything for good. Job lost his children, livestock and health. The beginning of the book makes it clear this is not punishment. God wants to prove something to Satan.

Job grieves his losses and asks questions. He argues with his so called friends who think the tragedies are his fault. But he is a good man. After his encounter with God, we see a changed Job. God has humbled and purified him. He says, "*My ears had heard of you, but now my eyes have seen you. Therefore I despise myself and repent in dust and ashes,*" (Job 42:5, NIV).

God had not meant Job's tragedies as punishment. The tragedies were Satan's idea. Yet God used them for good in Job's life to draw him into a more intimate and trusting relationship with God— to perfect his character. After this was accomplished, God blessed Job by restoring to him what Satan had stolen.

It intrigues me that Job knew God was at work. In the midst of his grief, he says, "*He knows the way that I take. When he has tried me, I shall come forth as gold"* (Job 23:8-10 RSV). Job trusted God even in the midst of intense grief.

I could definitely relate to these feelings. Early in my grief, before my first divorce, I felt the same way. Job 23 verse 10 was a great comfort then, and I referred to it in the song, "Comfort." But in my anger with God for not granting my requests, I temporarily forgot to trust that he was working for my good, refining me like gold

Rescued by Mercy

Tragedies are never God's idea. He is in the restoring business. Someone showed me Joel 2:25 many years ago. "*I will restore to you the years the locusts have eaten.*"

I believed God would restore everything Satan had robbed from me. Most of that promise has come true. Through it all, my Lord taught me to trust him better.

Through the book of Isaiah, God is trying to teach us to trust him. Everyone in the world is subject to God, therefore we should neither trust the other nations nor fear them. Since even God's judgment is mercy, we need fear only one thing—being outside of God's will where we make ourselves vulnerable to Satan.

Why does it take troubles and hardships to make people look to God? I think it is partly because people have a tendency to want to be their own god. When "our way" does not work, we look beyond ourselves for help. Hopefully, we look to God and learn to trust in and rely on Him.

Why does God want us to trust him? Because he loves us. Why is trust such a big deal to God? Neglecting our relationship with God and not paying attention to what he says, leads us to sin. Sin separates us from God, which is tragic. Eternal separation from God is hell. In contrast, trust connects us to God.

Many people feel the failures, dissension in relationships, frustrated plans, dryness, unfruitfulness, and confusion of our world. I was one of them, caught up in selfish desires.

When we are caught up in the things of the world, we cannot experience the full meaning of life. God can give this fullness, this abundant life, only when we put him first. Our heavenly Father knows what we need. When Jesus Christ is our heart's desire and single necessity, he begins to give our lives rich meaning and purpose.

Since I had been a Christian nearly 30 years, my situation was humiliating. At the time, I thought I was doing the right thing. I set out simply to show someone the love of Christ, yet I lost my way in the process.

Satan is so deceitful! Even now, I am not capable of sorting out which of my thoughts and actions were sinful rationalizations or deceptions of the devil and which were based on love and a desire to do God's will. All I know for sure is that God used those experiences to plow my heart so the seeds of trust and faith could grow.

I learned to trust God completely, to believe in his love for me. He refined my attitudes and brought me into a more intimate relationship with himself. During that dark time in my life, God also worked for my good through my job. A lady who had multiple sclerosis offered me a job as her nurse. Although only twenty-five years old, she was bedfast. After doing the necessary care each day, I would read to her from the Bible.

Someone had encouraged me to read five Psalms a day, starting with the day of the month, and every 30th Psalm thereafter. So she and I read these together. For four years we read five Psalms every day and talked about them. They became like friends to me.

One benefit was for her spiritual life. After a year, she told me, "I'm glad I have MS because now I know the Lord, and I didn't before."

This did my heart good. I didn't feel like such a failure. Besides, reading and talking about scripture brought the two of us into a deep friendship. The main benefit for me was that I became convinced God truly loved me and cared about my happiness. Never again would I doubt his love, although I often still don't understand why things happe as they do.

When we trust his love, we don't need to understand why things happen the way they do. If not for my divorce, I would not have needed this job. nor had this experience in learning to trust God.

Since God can and does use evil for good, let's be encouraged. God can take even our mistakes and sins and turn them into good. Perhaps we can even help others avoid slipping into a "miry pit." Maybe the good to come out of our mistakes will be that we can be used by God as instruments to bring others into a deeper relationship with himself.

By 2003, my faith and trust in God had grown to the point that I could trust God to work for good even while my third husband was dying of cancer. I kept telling myself, "*God is holy and righteous. He knows what he is doing and what he is doing is right.*"

Although I grieved his death, I trusted that God knew what wa best. My life had been a blessing to him and to his children for seventeen years. He was at peace with God when he died and is now perfectly healthy and happy in heaven, awaiting his loved ones. This knowledge gives me joy.

Prayer: *Thank you, LORD, for disciplining us for our good and setting us free. Use our mistakes for good. Enlighten our minds and draw our hearts into deeper love with you.*

In Jesus name, Amen.

Judith Vander Wege

God Alone is Perfectly Trustworthy

Isaiah, the evangelical prophet, knew he was called to be a watchman for his people — to warn them of approaching danger. Being compassionate, he was overcome with grief at the visions God shows him in Isaiah 21. He felt as if he were having labor pains.

Isaiah knew that the people of Judah would put their trust in Egypt and later in Babylon,, instead of paying attention to him and putting their trust in God. These were those nations which Isaiah foresaw would destroy Judah.

People are sometimes like that today. We may not be trusting in Babylon, but are we trusting in our material possessions? our intellect? our government? our employers? husbands? friends?

My mistake was that I looked to humans for fulfillment of my emotional needs and for my sense of self-worth. But only God can love us perfectly. Only God can be Jesus to us and make us feel worthwhile. He may work through other people, but it is idolatry to depend on other people instead of on God. No matter how loving and dependable a person is, there is always the possibility of him or her failing. Every human is a sinner.

Sinners are not trustworthy. Human beings are neither powerful enough nor faithful enough to be totally dependable, no matter how much they want to be. In contrast, God is powerful enough, loving enough, and totally faithful. "*All he does is just and good, and all his laws are right (Psalms* 111:7-9 The Living Bible).

Although we should not put our trust in other people, neither should we fear them. If we are afraid of wicked people, the following scriptures may be used as prayers: Psalm 37:10-11 and Psalms 35-36. God is sovereign and will deal with our enemies.

It is the responsibility of each Christian to be as trustworthy as possible. We can give ourselves completely to Jesus Christ, letting him have control of our lives. Then we thank him, praise him and obey him in all circumstances. In order to keep our promises and be trustworthy, sometimes we need to deny our desires.

It is natural to want to have our way but, out of love, we may need to give up our rights for a while. While it is normal and created within us to want to be loved, it is not right to use that desire as a justification for adultery, as I did.

Perhaps God wanted to use my love-hunger to draw me into a more intimate relationship with himself. Although he eventually did that, how much easier would it have been for me if I had steadfastly refused to commit adultery, even in my mind? It would have been better to look to Jesus for fulfillment and love.

Humans cannot and will not provide ultimate security for us. God will do this, if we are properly aligned with him. He loves us mo than we can ask or think. It is safe to surrender to him. It is safe to tru him with our interests and desires. He will either grant them or deny them, but it will always be what is best for us.

Psalm 37:4 says, "*Take delight in the Lord, and he will give yo the desires of your heart.*" Other encouraging verses are: Romans 8:2 Jeremiah 31:3, and Jeremiah 29:11-14.

Christ wants us to turn to our loving heavenly Father through his Holy Spirit. He will give us strength to be faithful even to those who fail us."

Each of three sections of Isaiah, chapters 13-23, 24-27, and

28-35 contain a lesson in trusting God. In the first, God alone is trustworthy. Therefore, it is foolish to look to human efforts for protection.

It's better to trust God than our money, insurance or retirement benefits. God wants us to use money wisely, not worship it. We should be good stewards of money as well as time, in obedience to his Word. We are blessed for a purpose, to be a blessing, to reach out to a hurting world, sacrificing our own desires when necessary in order to do his will. We belong to God and as we work for him we can depend on him to provide all we need. Our money as well as our abilities and time are to be used for his kingdom.

Isaiah's second lesson in trust, Isaiah 24-27, involves the devastation in the world. Tsunamis, wars and rumors of wars, starvation, unemployment and many other problems. Devastation has occurred in every age. Is there any hope for humanity? The Bible says, "Yes." God is our salvation.

Have you ever agonized over questions about life and death, purpose and meaning or truth? Job asked, "*Why didn't I die at birth?*

Why is a man allowed to be born if God is only going to give him a hopeless life of uselessness and frustration?" (Job 3:11, 23, TLB).

Although he doesn't hear answers to his questions, Job believes in God. Job finds it comforting that God knows what is going on.

King David also had questions: "*My God, my God, why have yo forsaken me...why do you refuse to help me?*" He concludes, "*God wil answer me and rescue me*." He decides he will praise the Lord and proclaim the wonderful things God has done (Psalms 22:1, 21b, 22-30 NIV).

When John the Baptist was in prison, he sent his disciples to ask Jesus, "*Are you he who is to come, or shall we look for another?*" (Matthew 11:3 RSV).

People continue to ask God heart-rending questions. Saint Augustine, Bishop of Hippo in North Africa in the 4th century, tells o his feelings. While tears poured from his eyes, he cried the words of Psalm 79, "*How long, Lord; wilt Thou be angry forever? Remember not our former iniquities.*"

Then he heard a child's singsong voice, "Take up and read." S he picked up the Bible and read where it fell open. In an instant "a lig of utter confidence shone in all my heart, and all the darkness of uncertainty vanished away," (Augustine's *Confessions,* 1020). His doubts, which had kept him from trusting the Lord, were gone.

After falling into Satan's trap, I felt I would never be of use to God again. When I reached the point where I could honestly say, "O Lord, take control," Jesus began to lead me out of the valley of despair and confusion.

Since that time, the Triune God has restored me. He brought me into a more intimate, loving relationship with himself. God convinced me he truly did love me and cared about my happiness. His purpose in judging and disciplining was to rescue me and draw me into a closer relationship with Himself.

The Lord is the answer to my deepest needs. As I trust his love, I do not need to understand why things happen as they do, but only how to obey him.

The whole purpose of our existence is to be in a covenant relationship with Almighty God. If we refuse to be in that covenant relationship, if we don't fit into his plans, why should he allow us to continue to exist? God mercifully waits for people to turn to him. He gives us extra chances.

In the midst of devastation and suffering, God is our hope, the answer to our problems. Since God is the answer, no other answers are essential. God created the earth and the entire cosmos; he has the right expect obedience. But sin constantly frustrates God's plan for this earth

If we turn to God in repentance and faith, we can experience peace, security and thankfulness even while, outwardly, we face the problems of a sinful world. Isaiah writes, "*He will keep in perfect peac all those who trust in him, whose thoughts turn often to the Lord!*" (Isaiah 26:3 TLB).

This type of trust is a total dependence on God who has delivered us. If we trust God like this, we will want our lives to mirror his.

Our Creator wants us to function the way we were created to function. If we live the way God intends, we will be a good witness of God's love. The believer longs for God's presence and wants God's w to be honored. When God's character is manifest in a believer's life, God's name is honored.

God loves his people but hates wickedness, especially in the people he has set free. Just as a gardener is diligent in weeding his garden, while paying little attention to weeds in a surrounding field,

God often disciplines Christians while it seems he is letting others get by with wickedness. "*The Lord disciplines him whom he loves, and chastises, every son whom he receives*" (Hebrews 12:6-7, RSV).

The results of God's training us will be fruitfulness. Even when our suffering is not due to God's discipline, yielding to him in trust is wise. He is always trustworthy and loving.

The following poem illustrates a heart yielded to God in trust:

Lord, Be the Ruler

Lord, be the ruler of my heart. I yield the throne to Thee.
I pray no selfishness nor pride, nor treasures that I see,
usurp the throne or take command to lead my flesh astray.
May you be King, and Lord of all that's in my life today.

Judith Vander Wege

Lord, be the ruler of my soul. My thoughts, so often wrong,

can keep me out of touch with you. The devil's pull is strong.

Yet, stronger still, your pull of love has led me here today

to ask you, Lord, to take control. Yes, be my King today.

Rescued by Mercy

Many of the people of Isaiah's time were foolish, not wanting to learn God's lessons. They refused to admit their sinfulness or to believe in the trustworthiness of Almighty God. For example, according to Isaiah 28:1-13, alcohol abuse was apparently a problem of the priests and prophets who should be giving clear guidance and teaching during the desperate times of impending destruction. Their resistance to Isaiah's teaching showed their unwillingness to surrender to the Lord.2:5 & 9). God's overall purpose in judging and disciplining people is to rescue them from Satan's trap and draw them into God's heart. Yet here are priests and prophets actually making use of one of Satan's tools for trapping people (alcohol).

According to Malachi 2:1-4, God is quite upset with priests who do not commit their hearts to honoring God by simple obedience. Those drunken leaders of Israel (Isaiah 28:7-8) complained that Isaiah treated them like children, with the same simple message over and over. Sometimes people are offended at the simplicity of the gospel message.

Judith Vander Wege

The well-educated Apostle Paul preached a simple gospel. For exampl
everyone is a sinner (Romans 3:23) therefore deserves death (Romans
6:23), but God offers the free gift of life in Christ Jesus. "By grace
you have been saved through faith; and this is not your own doing,
it is the gift of God, not because of works, lest any man should boast,"
(Ephesians 2:8-9, NIV.)

And here is John's simple gospel: "If we confess our sins,
he is faithful and just, and will forgive our sins and cleanse us from
all unrighteousness." (1 John 1:9 RSV).

To people who are trying to justify their actions and/or save
themselves (by spiritual activity or intellectual accomplishments),
this simple gospel feels foolish. But Isaiah's predictions of judgment
did come to pass. His messages of God's mercy for those who repent
have endured through the ages. The child he predicted to be born of a
virgin became our Redeemer and the "cornerstone" (Isa. 28:16-17)
of the church.

God alone is trustworthy. We can safely build on his foundati

Isaiah pleads with them again to listen: *God, our creator, can be trusted.* Just as he created the world with certain physical principles that are easy to discover, he also created spiritual principles. We ignore them only to our detriment. God's creation reflects his characteristics of truth, integrity, love, and faithfulness. Living according to these standards is an act of glad submission to our Creator. It is certainly foolish not to trust a trustworthy God.

Judith Vander Wege

Isaiah 29-30-31

The Lord's sadness comes through as he laments the phoniness of worship (Isaiah 29:13). The hope is that after judgment, the people will repent.

Isn't God great to give us a second chance? Have you ever needed one, as I have?

It is only a remnant that survived God's judgment on Jerusalem According to Psalm 51, God does not want sacrifice from us. He want a broken and contrite heart. True worship begins with repentance and the request for forgiveness and cleansing.

Even sincere Christians might attempt to manipulate God into granting prayers for selfish reasons rather than for worshiping and trusting him. We must examine our hearts: Do we truly love God for who he is, even if he does not answer our prayers the way we hope? Do we trust him even when we do not like or understand his answers

Isaiah presents the idea that God is like a potter and we are lik clay. God has the right to mold and use us however he wishes (Isaiah 29:16).

Judith Vander Wege

On My Father's Lap

In Isaiah 30-31, Isaiah continues to teach the people to trust in God, but instead they turn to Egypt for help. God warns them of the disastrous consequences, "*In repentance and rest is your salvation, in quietness and trust is your strength, but you would not*" (Isaiah 30:15) The words, "you would not" applied to me. I would not wait for God to handle the situation his way. I did not realize at the time that I was rebellious, because I believed God was leading me.

But a holy God will not lead us to a path that is clearly reveale in Scripture to be contrary to his will. It is frightening how the human mind can rationalize. I was looking "to Egypt" instead of to God to meet my needs for love and security. As a result, the adversity mentioned in Isaiah 30:20 came to me.

See how merciful God is! He "*longs to be gracious...to show you compassion,*" This astounded me...that he would still want me after I failed him!

When I repented in 1982 and learned to put my trust in the

Lord (i.e. "rested" in him), God became to me an intimate, loving Father. I used to think of him as a far-off Creator not much concerned with my personal life. I began to experience the truth of God's grace and guidance. He heard my weeping and cries for help and answered me. Throughout the adversity and affliction, he taught me who *He* is.

I was intrigued and comforted by the phrase, "*Your Teacher will not hide himself any more, but your eyes will see your Teacher.*" (Isaiah 30:20-21 RSV). This referred to *The* Teacher and my Savior, Jesus Christ. Therefore, I rejoiced at the promise that he would clearly teach me how to walk in his ways, like a mentor who cares for his pupil. He would no longer 'hide' from me but I would know him more personally.

My teacher taught me a great deal through the Holy Spirit in my private Bible study, especially in the Psalms and Isaiah. He also taught me through the little church I joined in 1982. Although only 100 members, they were so filled with the love of Jesus Christ. The worship services made me feel transported into God's throne room.

One time as the worship leader prayed, quoted Scripture and led the worshipful songs, I imagined Jesus picking me up tenderly as if I were an emotionally damaged child. He carried me across the threshold of the Holy of Holies and placed me in my loving father's lap. That was a big step toward healing.

I could not remember my earthly father holding me on his lap. Perhaps that was why I felt such a distance from God as father. But I knew Jesus loved me enough to die for me. Jesus also said, "*The Father himself loves you*" (John 16:27). Feeling my heavenly father hold me on his lap helped me learn to trust his love, to depend on him.

Other times with the people of that church were special, as we met in home meetings for prayer and Bible study. People would lay their hands on whomever wanted to be prayed for. They prayed like I had never heard before. As they prayed scripture, I felt as if God was speaking directly to my hurting heart. They were talking to their best friend and knew he would answer according to what was best. They prayed as if they truly cared about me. I began to believe God really loved me and wanted me to be happy.

How grateful I am for God's messages of mercy! Judgment is not God's last word for those who repent. He is a God of justice, but he is also a merciful God who loves to bring us back into his heart and restore to us all Satan has robbed from us.

When we trust and depend on God to supply our needs, delighting in his love and returning that love, we are more able to receive and appreciate the blessings God wants to give us.

In Chapters 31-33, Isaiah teaches the people to trust the Creator God rather than humans. It is foolish to trust the creature rather than the Creator.

Isaiah tells us a righteous king is coming (Isaiah 32:1-8). He will shelter and refresh. It seems as if Isaiah looks through a telephoto lens, zooming in on the Messianic Kingdom.

The first believers in Christ Jesus received the Holy Spirit when tongues of fire landed on their heads. Today, the Holy Spirit's presence may not be quite so dramatic. We receive the Holy Spirit when we receive Christ, when we repent and are baptized in the name of Jesus Christ. God is a gracious Father and his best gift is the Holy Spirit.

Isaiah's prayer in 33:2 and hopefully that of the people (including us) is that God will be gracious, will be our strength and our salvation. God loves to grant those requests. He has a rich treasure

of salvation, wisdom and knowledge stored up for us. The key to ope
up this stored treasure is "the fear of the Lord," (verse 6 NIV). When people finally acknowledge God is the Lord and give him reverent obedience, they find this treasure available.

Chapters 34 and 35 of Isaiah are a conclusion to the judgment in chapters 13-33. Isaiah has been tutoring the people with his lesson in trusting God: (1) God is sovereign. He loves people and hates wickedness. (2) God's purpose in disciplining us is to rescue us from Satan's trap and draw us into his heart. (3) God is trustworthy. He is the answer to our problems, so no other answers are essential.

My present husband's model train setup is called a 'pike.' He built mountains, railroads, a farm, a village, and other scenery, then put tiny people in it.

What if those tiny people shook their fists at him and said, "Why did you put me here? Why did you make me like this?"

What if a mouse climbed on the pike and messed things up? The train people looked to the other tiny people to protect them rathe than allowing the builder to protect them by capturing the mouse.

How silly! But isn't it just as silly for human beings to rebel at the God who created us and seek help from other people as weak and sinful as we are? Who Is the only one who can really help us?

In contrast, chapter 35 predicts the destiny of those who repent and trust God. Read it and note the difference. Which phrase would you most like to experience? I love the phrase, "*They will see the glory of the LORD, the splendor of our God*" (verse 2b). I want to see this glory myself. I also hope the Holy Spirit will sanctify and purify me so that others will see the glory of God working in me and through me. I want to reflect him.

The subtitle for Isaiah 35 is "Joy of the Redeemed." Only the redeemed can walk on the Way of Holiness mentioned in verse 8. "Redeemed" means "bought back." We belonged to God in the first place because he created us, then we were lost to him because of sin. But he bought us back through Christ's atonement on the cross.

Only God can ransom a soul from the penalty of sin. Only by faith in Christ (who paid the ransom) can one be made right with God.

Psalm103 assures me God forgives me and heals me. He redeemed me from the pit of hell and surrounds me with loving kindness.

Judith Vander Wege

Why does God love us so much that he wants to redeem us, to pour out his Holy Spirit on us and teach us to walk in his way? Perhaps it is because “God is love” (First John 4:8).

God desires to communicate with us. In order to break down the barriers between us and himself, he came to us in the person of Jesus Christ. He came to us to enable us to come to him. After we lear to walk in all his ways (to serve and love him with our whole heart), he enables us to go to others with love and compassion. That's how we can participate in his work and character.

The three tutoring sessions are completed. Soon the final exam will come.

Prayer:

Sovereign God, you hate wickedness because it destroys your beloved people. Thank you for rescuing us from evil and drawing us close to you. Thank you for teaching us that you are trustworthy.

In Jesus’ name we pray, Amen.

THE SOVEREIGNTY OF CHRIST

You are the mighty King, Master of everything.

Though you are gentle, you rule over all.

Why do you plead for me? Why did you bleed for me?

Why bother sending your call?

Your love has reached me and made me complete

so I could not resist all the love you did give.

Now I can worship you, Lord of the Universe

as in my heart you do live.

Jesus, I love you. I want to obey you

and live in a way that will glorify you.

How can I serve you best? Help me to stand the test.

Thank you for making me new.

You are my shepherd and you're my provider;

you have brought peace to this heart full of strife

I will obey you, for you are in charge of me.

You are the Lord of my life.

Judith Vander Wege

A Glimpse Into God's Heart

After the lessons in trust, we see how King Hezekiah does on the exam. Isaiah tells how Hezekiah reacts to an enemy threat and how he relates to God.

Hezekiah had watched his father, evil King Ahaz, rule for sixteen years before he died. He was old enough at 25 years old to know his father did wrong, particularly in his idolatry and child sacrifice. He had seen the judgment of the Lord because of Ahaz' sins. He knew his father chose to trust Assyria instead of God. Isaiah was undoubtedly a great influence on the young Hezekiah.

When Hezekiah began to reign, he made a covenant with the Lord and reinstated the tithe system and worship with its sacrificial system. Hezekiah continued to be a good king, and apparently tried to undo much of his father's disobedience. He destroyed the objects and places of idol worship and restored God's temple which his father had desecrated. Massive revival happened as the people returned to the Lord.

In the fourteenth year of his reign, Hezekiah began his final exam. Hezekiah had said “yes” to God from the beginning of his reign. But Sennacherib presented a new challenge.

Assyria was a great world power, and King Sennacherib expected everyone to be terrified of him. Yet Hezekiah dared to rebel against him, withholding tribute money. So the Assyrian King sent a message to try to scare Hezekiah into submission (see Isaiah 36:10).

Hezekiah first responded by tearing his robes, putting on sackcloth, and going to the temple to pray. He sent officials to Isaiah with news of the trouble and asked for prayer.

Isaiah gave him God’s message: “Do not be afraid... he shall hear a rumor, and return to his own land; and I will make him fall by the sword in his own land” (37:5-7).

Hezekiah believed Isaiah. He didn’t respond to Sennacherib’s threatening letters, but rather went to the temple and spread the letter out before God in prayer. He trusted God. You can read Hezekiah’s beautiful prayer in Isaiah 37:14–20.

God said Sennacherib had mocked and insulted The Holy One of Israel. God promised to defend Jerusalem. Later, in the temple of his own god, the arrogant Sennacherib was assassinated by his own sons (36-38).

Hezekiah had passed this test victoriously. He trusted God and God came through for him.

Later God gave Hezekiah another test to "*try him and to know all that was in his heart*" (Second Chronicles 32:31). Babylonian envoys came to visit. Hezekiah had the opportunity to tell the Babylonians about his wonderful God, but he gave in to pride. He showed them everything in his treasury. Hezekiah failed this test. However, when Hezekiah humbled himself, the Lord showed him mercy.

Like Hezekiah, most of us need to learn an ongoing lifestyle of trust in God, not for selfish reasons or to get out of crises. True trust involves a deeply committed relationship with our heavenly Father. Manipulative prayers only to see our needs met are not appropriate.

Just as the compassionate God considered Hezekiah valuable enough to teach him lessons in trust, so he considers us valuable as well. Chapter 40 and the next few chapters were the chapters so intimately pertinent to me three decades ago. Although I would always regret my lack of trust in my Savior and the resultant disobedience, God brought me into his heart through these messages of mercy, into willing obedience and joy in relationship with him.

These chapters, written one hundred years before Jerusalem fell and the Babylonians took the people into exile in Babylon, answer the questions people are bound to have during their punishment (their exile): 1. *Is God not strong enough to defeat my enemies?*

2. Has my failure to trust God and obey him completely separated me from God and his purpose for my life?

3. Has God abandoned me?

Isaiah answers by proclaiming God's grace. Grace motivates people to trust God.

When I read Isaiah 40:1-2, it felt like a healing balm poured over my aching heart. These verses indeed gave me a glimpse of God's heart. I was reassured He still loved me and that he was eager to end my strife.

I knew about the message of judgment. Now I learned the message of hope. God made it possible for me to follow the right roa

Deliverance comes only from God's intervention. God had a plan for me and prepared a way. Jesus my Savior was my way back t the road of holiness.

God keeps his promises.

Isaiah 40:12-17 emphasizes the awesome greatness of God, the Creator of the universe. Since he is such a powerful Creator of the whole cosmos, we should be able to trust him with our lives.

“Have you not known? Have you not heard? The LORD is the everlasting God, the Creator of the ends of the earth. He does not faint or grow weary; his understanding is unsearchable. He give power to the faint, and to him who has no might he increases strength... but they who wait for the LORD shall renew their strengt they shall mount up with wings like eagles, they shall run and not be weary, they shall walk and not faint” (Isaiah 40:27-31 RSV).

I love the picture of soaring like eagles. The verb translated “hope” in the NIV is translated “wait” in other translations. To “wait on God is to “live in confident expectation of his action on our behalf. It is to refuse to run ahead of him in trying to solve our problems for ourselves” (Oswalt, 448).

As the Life Application Bible explains: “We all need regular times to listen to God. Waiting on the Lord is expecting his promised strength to help us rise above life’s distractions and difficulties. Listening to God helps us to be prepared for when he speaks to us, to be patient when he asks us to wait, and to expect him to fulfill the promises found in his Word”(p. 1027).

The Lord is indeed trustworthy. We will be blessed as we surrender to him.

Judith Vander Wege

Personal Applications of Isaiah 40

Isaiah knew God's heart. Just as the glorious vision Isaiah had seen so many years earlier changed his life, so our lives can be changed when we see God as he really is.

Like Isaiah, I needed to be cleansed and purified before I could be effective in God's Kingdom. First, I needed to realize "*Woe is me,"* not in a self-pitying way but rather admitting my sin. At first, I rationalized my disobedience, feeling there were inescapable reasor for my adultery. Later, when God showed me my heart, I saw it was contaminated with wrong attitudes which had been present long befo I broke my marriage vows.

As a teenager, I was proud of the fact that I was not like other teens who became rebellious. And, during my first marriage, I believ I was a good wife who loved and respected my husband and took wonderful care of my children. I tried to treat everyone the way Jesu would want me to treat them, and I prided myself on nonconformity the wrong ways of the world.

However, I became convicted about failing God by my lack of trust in him. Other sinful attitudes came into focus: bitterness, resentment, pride, jealousy, self-righteousness, rebelliousness, and most of all—unfaithfulness to my Savior, Jesus Christ. Although he was faithful in helping me during the heartache of a failing marriage, I disobeyed him. I listened to half-truths and considered God unfair. In essence, I called God a liar when I asked him, "Where's the abundant life you promised in John 10:10?"

By letting emotions take control and embracing the 'forbidden fruit,' I unwittingly put myself on the throne instead of the Lord, who deserved to be there. As all this became clear, I felt like Isaiah, "Woe is me! For I am lost!" The Holy Spirit convicted me. I wanted Jesus Christ back on the throne of my heart, so I repented and asked forgiveness. Isaiah1:18 reminds us, "*Though your sins are like scarlet, they shall be as white as snow; though they are red like crimson, they shall be like wool.*"

Forgiveness and justification are instantaneous as soon as we repent. But the purification (sanctification) will take a while. It is a process.

Judith Vander Wege

After I received forgiveness, I still needed to learn to trust in God's love more completely. I needed purification.

In God's sight, we are like precious gold. Much is done to gold before it becomes pure. The ore is ground to free the gold particles. These are amalgamated, heated in a furnace, soaked in cyanide, melted and cast into gold bars. To change the gold bars into gold leaf for decorating precious jewelry, the steps include: flattening cutting, beating with a hammer and repeating this process for four hours until light shines through the transparent sheets.

It is no fun to go through the purification process but Job write "*He knows the way that I take; when he has tested me, I will come for as gold*"(Job 23:10 NIV).

My purification process seemed to take longer than Job's. Or maybe I "wandered in the wilderness" as a consequence of my sin. Although God had forgiven me, I continued to hurt. For years it felt like there was a gaping hole in my chest. Realizing I had failed God, who truly loved me, added to the past heartache and present pain.

In contrast, Isaiah 40:1-2 seemed like a wonderful oasis I longed to reach, "Comfort...warfare is ended...double forgiveness...."

It was like a glimpse inside the loving heart of God. I wanted to be there with God, but felt I did not deserve it.

Alone in my mobile home, I spent hours studying the Bible. At work, I read to my private-duty patient from the Psalms. Gradually, the Lord convinced me his offer of forgiveness was really for me. As I cast myself on Jesus Christ, knowing I was totally dependent on him life and health and every good, I began to feel I would reach this oasis. Comfort washed over my heart. Then, like Isaiah after he had been cleansed, I wanted to tell everyone about this awesome God.

It must pain God to discipline his children. But when the discipline is over, all he wants to do is comfort them, reassure them of forgiveness, love them and let them know forgiveness is complete.

God’s comfort leads us to trust him more. Then, in turn, we can comfort others. We are blessed to be a blessing.

Judith Vander Wege

Comfort and Hope For God's Chosen Instruments

Listen—The grand court case is about to begin. Let's decide the point at issue between us—**Is God in charge or not?**

Isaiah wrote for future readers. In about 150 years, Cyrus would come on the historical scene of history. If God was not all-powerful, could he bring "*one from the east whom victory meets at every step?*" (Isaiah 41:2). If God was not omniscient, could he predict what Cyrus would do? Were idols powerful enough and omniscient enough?

Cyrus, King of Persia, founder of the great Persian empire, did capture Babylon in 539 B.C. He made the declaration that the Jews were free to return to their homeland and rebuild the house of their Lord in Jerusalem.

The fact that God stirred up Cyrus and that God still continues to direct the affairs of men, is given as a proof of God's Sovereignty. Pagan nations make idols and expect them to help. How ridiculous! According to Isaiah, God is in charge.

Prophecies often have double meanings. God had previously called Abraham to be the founder of the Israelite nation (Genesis 12:1-4). If God was powerful enough and had enough authority to call a man away from his "*country, his kindred, and his father's house*" to go to a strange land, then to bless him and make his name great, developing a whole nation from him, didn't that prove he had more power than idols?

Isaiah's prophecy must have also encouraged the captives later in Babylon to believe God and learn to trust him. They needed to decide "Who's in charge?" So do we. If God is omnipotent and omniscient, shouldn't we allow him to be in charge of our lives? He has chosen to redeem us and to use all who yield to his will.

I felt reassured that the promises to the Israelites apply to all who believe in God. Therefore God says to me, "You are my servant, and I have not rejected you."

Since I felt so strongly convicted of my sin, I drank in this reassurance. *God has not rejected me! I can still be his servant—his instrument, even if I'm still in exile.*

Although God had lifted me out of the 'pit,' I still felt like I was in 'exile' — in a sort of wilderness. I needed more of God's grace. God often gave this grace to me through music. One example is the song, "Comfort" song, (see chapter one). Another song it seemed as if God was singing to me, was "I Will Restore You Now."

Although I used to feel insignificant and useless in God's kingdom, I have become convinced God has chosen me to be one of his instruments. You can be, too.

Over the years, a desire grew inside me to share the songs that helped me grow. As I ministered in nursing homes, retirement homes and church, I discovered the songs also spoke to their hearts. In God's economy, no one is blessed only for his own sake. I hope God will continue to use my music and writing for future generations. He is a creative, wonderful God. What a privilege to be one of his instruments of grace.

As God kept speaking to my heart through His Word. Isaiah 41:10-13 became a lifeline to me. I memorized verse 10 and used it as a weapon against attacks of fear. "*Fear not, for I am with you, be not dismayed, for I am your God; I will strengthen you, I will help you, I will uphold you with my victorious right hand.*"

As the full consciousness of my sinful heart came into focus, fear overwhelmed me. *I've let emotions rule me. I know now I cannot trust them. Will I continue to be deceived? How can I make decisions wisely? How do I know whether I'm rationalizing or not? Will God ever be able to use me again?*

The reason we should not fear is because God is with us. If God is in control, he will defeat our enemies. If we fear and reverence the Lord, he will protect and help us.

While God purified me through my struggles, I continued to search desperately for answers to my questions.

Humbled by God's mercy, I realized the consequences of my sin could have been much worse. God's gentle discipline encouraged me that he would also keep his good promises. I had believed John 3:16 since I said 'Yes' to Jesus as a child. But somewhere along the way, I lost my first love for him. That is why I lost my way and took this road through the wilderness. It took many years to get out of the wilderness.

Meanwhile, God's presence became vividly real to me

through repeating the words of Isaiah 41. I also looked forward to the day promised in verses 11-12, "*Look, all who were angry at you will be ashamed and humiliated; your adversaries will be reduced to nothing and perish. When you look for your opponents, you will not find them; your enemies will be reduced to absolutely nothing.*"

I was in the thick of spiritual battle. Satan wanted to destroy me both physically and emotionally, although he had already lost the battle spiritually. It meant so much to know the Lord my God held my right hand.

But I still felt like the insignificant worm which God promised to help. Earthworm activity aerates and mixes the soil. It is constructive to mineralization and nutrient uptake by vegetation. Because a high level of organic matter mixing is associated with soil fertility, an abundance of earthworms is beneficial to the organic gardener. This analogy shows how God chooses insignificant people to be his instruments.

The Lord says he will not forsake the needy but will answer them and turn their wilderness into a beautiful place, (Isaiah 41: 17-20). Now I can see he has done this for me as well.

Prayer:

Lord, you are our strength and provider. You are the One who knows all the answers to our questions and our lives. You are Almighty God, creator and the one who sustains our universe. Yet, you have chosen us to be your instruments. I am honored or privileged or delighted or committed to put you first. You are my all in all! Amen.

Judith Vander Wege

God's Chosen Servant is the Light

Isaiah 42:1-9 is the first of Isaiah's "servant songs," which describe the ministry of this special, ideal servant who will bring relief for the oppressed. Isaiah is referring to the Messiah, Jesus.

Even if we know Jesus, we do not always choose to walk in his light. Sometimes, we let our old natures get the upper hand. Blindness may afflict us, and Satan may deceive us. As a consequence of rebellion, we may fall into his traps.

Even then he promises to lead us and guide us, to not forsake us (Isaiah 42:16). What a merciful God!

By the Holy Spirit, God impressed Isaiah's words on my heart. Since I could not see or hear God clearly, I had failed to fulfill God's purpose for me. I thought I was committed to him. Yet, I had blindly followed the deceiver.

I deserved the Lord's fury and wrath. God understood how I felt. He knew how desperate was my situation. Since I stepped outside his will, it was hopeless to get out of that pit by myself— hopeless to fulfill the purpose for which I was born.

Rescued by Mercy

I imagined the following vignette:

Your Only Hope

"Look at my Son! Look at my Son!" the Father's urgent voice pleads.

"Why should I look at your son?" yells the man in the pit, his eyes blazing and his fists clenched. "So I can see how shameful I am in comparison? So I can admire your pure, sinless specimen of humanity? You think you're so smart. All you care about is how great he is. You don't even care that I'm rotting down here."

The Father's eyes brim with tears. His voice trembles as he replies, "No, you misunderstand. I want you to look at my Son so you can see his nail-pierced hand reaching out to rescue you from the pit. I want you to look at my Son because I love you. He is your only hope."

As I continued reading in Isaiah, I saw God's mercy more clearly. In my mind's eye, I saw Jesus weeping for me. I realized he cared how much I hurt and wanted me to reach out for his rescuing hand. I began to hope, *he wants to rescue me and forgive me. He loves me!*

God fulfilled his promise for me. In spite of my rebellion and blindness, God never forsook me. He faithfully led me through my wilderness and guided me until he turned my darkness into light and made my paths smooth again.

Prayer: *Father, we praise you for your out-stretched hand of mercy, for giving us hope. Thank you for your messages of mercy through Isaiah. Thank you, Jesus, for faithfully carrying out your role as the Suffering Servant who died to rescue us. Thank you, Holy Spirit, for making these truths clear to us. We praise you Holy, Triune God.*

Amen.

Passing through the Waters

"When you pass through the waters, I will be with you; and through the rivers, they shall not overwhelm you; when you walk through fire, you shall not be burned and the flame shall not consume you"(Isaiah 43:2, RSV).

What a promise! I read it and reread it, hoping it applied to me—that God was with me and protecting me. I felt as if I were passing through deep waters, fighting the current in a spiritual sense. I hoped, yet I wondered—why would God want to be with people whose own disobedience got them into trouble?

Is the Lord qualified to be our God? Does he have a right to tell us what to do—to expect us to pay attention to him? Does he expect us to believe he can help us in our "robbed and plundered" condition?

According to Isaiah 43:1, God has certain qualifications. He is the one who *created you, formed you, redeemed you, (bought you back) called (or summoned) you*. Wouldn't you expect something you created to function in the way you created it to function?

As my present husband worked to make his HO train setup, he created a scene on wide shelves that filled most of the space in our shed. He worked hard to create mountains and scenery, villages and farms. The little people that fit in the scenes were less than one inch tall, each standing or sitting beside a small house, store, farm building or hill. What if they were alive? Would they wonder how they got there? Would they shake their tiny fists at their maker saying, "Why did you put me on a farm instead of in town? Why did you let me fall into this pit?" or "Why am I in this family?"

It is just as preposterous to shake our fists at God.

Yet, even if we have done so, the LORD promises to be with those whom he has redeemed. Even if our own disobedience has gotten us into trouble, he loves us. God is too good to be unkind. He is holy and righteous. He knows what is right to do and he does it.

Isaiah 43 emphasizes God's mercy. He does not give up on us, but, like a loving father, he disciplines us when we need it. Christians *will* suffer heartaches, difficulties and trials, however.

Rescued by Mercy

What could be some modern ways that people are, “sent into exile?” Our heartaches, illnesses and separations from loved ones are not always because of our sins, but they could be.

When I was going through the most difficult time of my life, I felt as if I were drowning in heartache and struggling against an opposing current. The Holy Spirit made it clear to me through Isaiah 43:1 that I belonged to God. He would be with me through the rough times. He is always with me. This was so encouraging. Jesus also said he would always be with me.

The reason the Lord redeems us (“buys us back”) is that he considers us precious and honored. He loves us. In my drought of self-esteem, I clung to those words. Isn’t his love astounding, considering how God’s people (both Israel and us) broke his heart with their (our) rebellion?

In a small way, God called me to be one of his spokesmen, (as a writer) to bring God’s messages to the world. Israel was not serving God obediently, yet Israel did bring God’s Word to the world in the form of a baby. (John 1:12)

All this truth gives me hope that I can fulfill my purpose.

Judith Vander Wege

The more we realize our sinfulness and inability to live perfect lives, the more we love the Lord and appreciate his grace. After my "Teacher," (Jesus Christ), opened my eyes and ears to his will, I did not want any idolatry in my life. It took adversity and affliction to get me to that point. We can trust God to do what is best when we ask him to take control of our lives.

Isaiah 43:8-17 sounds like another courtroom scene. God calls Israel to be his witnesses.

God is Triune. Therefore, Father, Son, and Holy Spirit have fellowship with each other and the angels. They do not *need* fellowship with us. Nor is it a matter of competition. It is simply agape love, love generously given for our sake. Love is the very essence of God's being.

God does us the tremendous favor of blotting out our sins. He asks us to pay attention to him, even argue with him if necessary. Those who keep on ignoring him and not obeying him will end up in destruction — by their own choice.

Prayer: Thank you, Lord, for calling us into relationship with you. Thank you for promising to be with us in our trials. Thank you, Jesus, for being my teacher as well as Savior. Amen.

Judith Vander Wege

You May Know The Redeemer

"But now listen...This is what the Lord says...

he who made you in the womb, and who will help you;

Do not be afraid...I will pour out my Spirit on your offspring,

and my blessing on your descendants.

They will spring up like grass in a meadow,

like poplar trees by flowing streams.

One will say, "I belong to the Lord;"

another will call himself by the name of Jacob;

still another will write on his hand, 'The Lord's'

and will take the name Israel. (Isaiah 44:1-5).

When I was going through my wilderness, the first verses of Isaiah 44 seemed especially comforting and encouraging. They made me feel as if God held me on his lap and gently talked with me. He gave me promises for both me and for my children. My heart was the "dry, thirsty ground," and I rejoiced in his promise to send his Sp on my descendants.

When God pours out his Spirit on a person, the life may be transformed. Think of the Apostle Paul, Christ's disciples, Zacchaeus, and Mary Magdalene in the New Testament. Or consider Nicky Cruz (*Run Baby Run*), and Alexandra Zamora (*Oasis for the Nations*) as examples of transformed lives.

Why does God demand to be Number One? Because he loves us so much and knows it is best for us to worship *only* him. We become like what we worship. If we worship the true God, we will take on his characteristics. God is good, loving, merciful, righteous, kind, faithful, just and patient. We can have those qualities, too.

In Isaiah 44:21-28 God pleads with his people to remember. He is not casting away his people because of their sin. Rather, he is begging them to return to him. He longs to forgive them (and us). With the intimacy restored, God recounts what he has done and what he will continue to do as Redeemer.

In Isaiah 46, God goes on to call the house of Jacob "stubborn-hearted, you who are far from righteousness...." One might expect God to give up on them.

Yet in his mercy, God wants to "grant salvation" — to *give* people his righteousness. We cannot be right with God just by doing the right things. But we can agree with God that we are hopelessly lost. We can believe in the truth about Christ that all our sins have been forgiven. Accepting this truth is what makes us right with God. In our ongoing life of faith, God does not want us to deal with obstacles in our *own* power, but to surrender to him and trust in his promises.

Affliction can bring about a transformation in a person's life. Until a person is afflicted, there's no reason to want to change. When a person is in trouble, he or she will more likely cry out to God for help.

When the disciple Peter walked on water in response to Jesus' call, he did not cry out "Save me!" until he started sinking. Jesus allowed him to start to sink because he was teaching him dependence on his Lord. This was an essential skill he would need for the rest of his life. We can also learn how to depend completely on our Savior.

Imagine God is saying to you, "Believe in me. I made you. I have provided a way to rescue you."

Rescued by Mercy

God tries to reason with us. He is trying to teach us what is best for us. He can direct us in how to live our lives. He cares deeply about the choices we make and the directions our lives take.

We also can be released from the traps that enslave us. In Jesus Christ, God has provided freedom and forgiveness for past sins. The Eternal Spirit took on flesh. The Creator of the Universe is able to do the impossible and transform people's lives by reconciling them to himself.

Because I have been redeemed and forgiven, I can be an ambassador and appeal to people to accept God's love. (2 Cor. 5:19). My bond of guilt has been canceled.

God is able to make our lives full of joy, peace and purpose. He is waiting for us to respond to his offer.

Prayer: *Dear Lord, Thank you for redeeming me and transforming my life into one of peace, joy and hope. I pray you will remove everything in my life that hinders the progress and success of the gospel. Use me as your ambassador. Let your divine grace be victorious over all opposition. In Jesus's name, Amen.*

Judith Vander Wege

The Suffering Servant

"*The Lord called me from the womb...made my mouth like a sharp sword,...and he said to me, 'You are my servant, Israel, in whom I will be glorified*'" (Isaiah 49:1-3 RSV).

How can someone be called before he is born? How can a mouth be like a sword and a person like an arrow?

According to the commentator, this servant is the Messiah whom Isaiah previously foretold. Israel is unable to restore herself to God, and neither could an ordinary human.

The first Servant Song (Isaiah 42) says this ideal servant will bring relief for the oppressed. He will have God's Holy Spirit, be righteous, and bring justice. He will compassionately reach out to us after dying to rescue us.

The Lord said he would make his servant to be a covenant.

Jesus established this new covenant at the last supper with his disciples.

Rescued by Mercy

After the suffering servant freed the captives, he was a good shepherd to them. This message gave them hope of deliverance. The same is true today for those who are freed from the captivity of sin. Freedom from captivity is a wonderful thing.

Isaiah encourages us by reminding us God would no more forget us than a mother would forget her baby. He has even tattooed our names on his palms (Isaiah 49:15-16).

God has qualities of strength and compassion. He fought against my enemies (which were spiritual and emotional) and led me out of captivity. God is trustworthy.

The servant will have character qualities of wisdom, encouragement, being teachable and submissive to the Lord. He is brave, meek, dignified, grateful for help, determined to complete his purpose and trusting in God. The Sovereign Lord will rescue his people from sin through the obedience of his Servant.

After Jesus rose from the dead, the good news of salvation spread throughout the whole world. Likewise, if we submit to the will of our heavenly father, God can use us for good purposes. Each disciple of Christ who wishes to make a positive difference chooses to let Jesus Christ be Lord. When we choose to submit to him in obedience, he enables us to be effective in God's Kingdom.

God wants to help us, to save us. But he is holy and pure. We cannot hold onto our sin and have a relationship with him at the same time. But he knows we are unable to cleanse ourselves from sin. That is why he provided the Messiah, Jesus, to take away the sin that separates us from God and restore us to an intimate relationship with God our Father.

God did not forget me. He helped me out of my troubles. As a Christian writer, he has put his words in my mouth, and hidden me in the shadow of his hand (Isaiah 51:16).

Jesus is the predicted Messiah, the suffering servant, which Isaiah 52–53 describes. No one in Nazareth except Mary and Joseph expected him, as a growing boy, to become anything special. Yet he accomplished the work that God had promised and predicted thousands of years earlier. Jesus, God's suffering servant was lifted up and exalted, first on the cross, then in resurrection and ascension.

What great love the Triune God has for us, that he would go to such a great extent to rescue us! God himself died for us so that we do not have to suffer spiritual death because of our sin. What an awesome, merciful God! Thus Isaiah, the evangelical prophet, insists that God has not given up on his people because of their sin. Rather, he has planned a way to bring them back to him. These words, fromWillam R. Newell's hymn, praise God for that wonderful plan:

At Calvary

"Oh, the love that drew salvation's plan.

Oh, the grace that brought it down to man.

Oh, the mighty gulf that God did span

At Calvary.

Mercy there was great, and grace was free.

Pardon there was multiplied to me.

There my burdened soul found liberty

At Calvary.

Prayer: *Thank you, Jesus, for being obedient to your Heavenly Father, for becoming my Savior and my Redeemer. I choose to be obedient to you. Please give me strength and wisdom to do so. Amen.*

Judith Vander Wege

Restoration and Hope For a Disgraced Woman

Israel was the "disgraced, barren woman, the widow, the divorced one" of Isaiah 54. The basic problem was alienation from God's presence. But humans never need to be separated from Him again. The love and peace God offers are forever.

All who believe in the Lord are part of his "bride." We can know these verses were written directly for us. We have been redeemed by the Servant/Messiah. Now we must continually choose to live under the terms of his covenant in order to experience its blessings.

I felt as if these verses were written specifically for me, because I was also a disgraced woman. I found many portions of Isaiah 54 meaningful. During my first marriage, verse one touched my heart. Each month for the first three years, I cried when I was not pregnant.

Then we adopted a baby girl and two years later, a baby boy. These brought joy and satisfied my need for children, but I still wished I could experience pregnancy and nursing a baby. Finally, after eleven years of marriage, I became pregnant and gave birth to a baby boy. God granted my desires. What joy these children brought!

However, when the divorce happened five and a half years after my younger son's birth, I was essentially barren again because my children left with their dad, 1000 miles away.

Isaiah commands the barren one to sing (Isaiah 54:1). How could I sing after experiencing divorce and bereavement--- I, who had been so strongly opposed to divorce, and then experienced another divorce within three years? Yet, the second half of this verse felt like a promise to me that I would someday feel like singing again. I began to hope that my life would no longer be fruitless.

I didn't know what to make of that promise other than things would get better. But years later, I gained four step-children through a remarriage. After that husband died of cancer seventeen years later, I gained three more step-children through another remarriage. Now we cannot keep up with the twenty-five grandchildren's birthdays.

While I was going through the emotional trauma of those two divorces and the disastrous consequences of my wrong choices, these words were like salve to my soul: "*Do not be afraid; you will not suffer shame. Do not fear disgrace; you will not be humiliated. You will forget the shame of your youth and remember no more the reproach of your widowhood. For your Maker is your husband*"(4-5).

One day, early in my third marriage, the mistakes of the past were especially painful to me before we saw a double rainbow. It was beautiful and reminded me of Isaiah 54.

God was telling me through that rainbow that he had "brought me back." He had forgiven me and was no longer angry. The rest of the chapter assured me he would restore me and build me up. He would teach my children and give them peace. He would establish me in righteousness and keep me safe.

Isaiah 55 was also extremely comforting to me. God invited me to come and drink of the River of Life. He wanted to be my sustenance. I became increasingly thirsty for the scriptures, so I accepted his invitation.

Rescued by Mercy

All people are encouraged to seek the Lord. I sensed the Holy Spirit telling me to seek a deeper relationship with Jesus Christ, to trust that he knew what was best. I learned that the deeper, more intimate relationship with Jesus is the abundant life which he promised in John 10:10.

Then in Isaiah 55:12-13, what precious promises! These verses are a glorious song of victory, either in this life or in heaven,

"*You shall go out in joy and be led forth in peace.*"

I felt this joy because the Lord had restored me to that intimate relationship with himself."I Will Restore You Now," expresses my convictions after studying several chapters of Isaiah. God spoke to my heart and said, "You are my precious child. I love you so, my child. I will restore you now."

I praise God for his restoration of relationship with me.

Even though the work of making a person right is God's doing, righteous living is a requirement for the servants of God. It is not enough for us to say "once saved, always saved" and then not bother about obedience. However, this righteous living is only possible through the grace of God. We are expected to obey the Lord.

Judith Vander Wege

God's main concern is that we believe his Word that says his grace is a free gift. We do not have to work our way into God's favor. This type of righteousness is an act of love, service, and worship. Obedience to God shows we are members of the covenant community. The Spirit of Christ in us enables us to do right.

All people are welcome to bind themselves to the Lord, not just the Jews or "perfect" people. Isaiah warns the leaders of Israel that if they continue being greedy, self-centered, and power-hungry, the flock will be overtaken by spiritual enemies. Some leaders seemed to feel God asked too much that they let him control their lives and surrender to him in trust. Whether we are leaders or not, all Christians have an influence on other people. If we do not let God control our lives, that influence may not be good.

God knows we are unable to live righteous lives in our natural state and He is a merciful God. All we need to do is recognize our need for God's forgiveness —turn to him, accept his forgiveness, and be willing to turn away from our sin. He will then give us the power needed to do this. He will heal our sin-sick souls, guide us and restore comfort to us as we rely on him. This is certainly good news.

God even gives people the *desire* to turn to him. He heals them so they are able to desire righteousness and ask God for help. Through a loving relationship with God, the by-products of righteousness and justice are developed in our lives.

God wants to give all people a changed nature, but he does not force himself on people. The wicked refuse to admit their sinfulness and their need for a Savior. They refuse to turn to God and away from their sin.

Prayer: *Lord, I thank you for forgiveness. Thank you for giving it freely to those who believe in you, so we can rest in you. Amen.*

Judith Vander Wege

Wrong versus Right Worship

Isaiah says something is wrong with the religion of God's people who were disobedient to God by oppressing their workers.

God is not interested in empty, outward-only rituals. He wants our hearts. The people were fasting, not to express gratitude and submission to God, but to manipulate him to do what they wanted him to do. This does not please God. God's blessing is given freely to those who are in an unbroken covenant relationship with him. The evidence of this covenant relationship is ethical behavior. God wants people to stop oppressing the poor (treat them fairly and give them what they earn), to not be greedy or selfish, to help people, to be light, and to delight in the Lord (Isaiah 58:6).

God is always ready to offer mercy to those who will repent of their sin. His mercy gives the gift of repentance so we are able to repent. Then he gives us the ability to obey. After I was restored to fellowship with God, Jesus ruled in my heart.

In Isaiah 61, the work of the promised Messiah is made clear. He was anointed "*to preach good news to the poor, bind up the brokenhearted, proclaim freedom for the captives, and release for the prisoners, proclaim the year of the Lord's favor and the day of vengeance of our God, to comfort all who mourn, and provide for those who grieve in Zion—to bestow on them a crown of beauty instead of ashes, the oil of gladness instead of mourning, and a garment of praise instead of a spirit of despair…* (Isaiah 61:1-3 NIV).

After I had received the Lord's good news, my broken heart began to mend. I became free from bondage to my emotions, especially resentment. God comforted me, and I began to develop an attitude of praise.

Prayer: *Thank you, Lord Jesus, Almighty God, for defeating the sin that used to reign in me. I praise you that you have done what the law could not do. You have set me free from failure as well as unrighteousness. Now shine through me for your glory. Amen.*

Judith Vander Wege

Prophecies Culminate in Christ

In chapter 63, Isaiah talks about God as a warrior ready to defeat sin. Those who allow him to make them righteous will be his true servants to call the nations to worship the righteous God. Redemption and continued sin cannot co-exist. Therefore, the sin must be destroyed before the person can be free.

Grieving the Holy Spirit causes him sorrow. Can you grieve those who do not love you? You might anger them or make them want to stay away from you, but grieving indicates relationship, actual or desired.

Here is where the gospel becomes clear as such an *amazing grace*. Even if we, who were once walking closely with the Lord, have dragged his name in the mud by our rebellion and wrong choices, God still desires our fellowship. He loves us and calls us back.

His Spirit is grieved not only because of what we are doing, but also because of how we are hurting inside. He loves us and knows the only way for us to have joy and peace is for our sins to be forgiven and washed away. He wants us to have the joy of living righteous lives through the power of his Holy Spirit.

When I wrote the song called “Through the Valley,” I wanted to give a testimony of how God had worked in my life. After my loneliness, depression, grieving and wrong choices, I finally cried out to God and sought him in his Word. When I learned to cling to Jesus and trusted him to set me free, allowing him back on the throne of my heart, then I could praise him and grow into the joy of his salvation. Jesus had not abandoned me, but rather was always with me, even in my valleys.

In a Christian's spiritual walk, it is not unusual to go through a dark valley. Whether this valley is grief, illness, or some other tragedy, it is tempting to feel we are all alone. We are not sure God sees us or cares about our happiness. But think of this chorus as Jesus singing to you:

Through the Valley

I felt so all alone, so lost and far from home.

I looked not forward to another day.

Judith Vander Wege

I longed for Christ to come.

I said, “Please take me home!”

Then Jesus lovingly showed me the way:

Chorus

“You must go through the valley to get to the other side.

It's lonesome in that valley, but I will be your guide.

I know you feel I'm far away, that I don't hear you when you pray,

but even in your valley, I am always close to you.”

The grief I could not bear without someone to care,

though Jesus promised he'd be by my side.

I could not feel his love; I wanted flesh and blood

and so I took a road that led nowhere.

Then I cried out to God. I sought him in his word.

He said, “My precious child, you are my own.

You need to cling to me. Trust me to set you free.

Just hold my hand and I will lead you home.”

Rescued by Mercy

Chorus: "You must go through the valley to get to the other side.

It's lonesome in that valley, but I will be your guide.

I know you feel I'm far away, that I don't hear you when you pray,

but even in your valley, I am always close to you."

So now I praise His name. My Savior, still the same,

has led me forward through the sun and rain.

He's brought me close to Him. He's taught me how to win.

By trusting Him, I've learned to grow through pain.

Chorus

"You must go through the valley to get to the other side.

It's lonesome in that valley, but I will be your guide.

I know you feel I'm far away, that I don't hear you when you pray,

but even in your valley, I am always close to you.

Yes, even in your valleys, I am always close to you."

***

Judith Vander Wege

In chapter 63, Isaiah calls us back to our first love, into intimacy with the Lord. God wants us to cling to him in trust and let him lead us.

I loved Jesus above all as a child and teen, but in my early adulthood, in sneaky ways I did not recognize, other things or people began to take supremacy.

During my journey back to the Lord, I was convicted by this verse, "*Yet I hold this against you: You have forsaken your first love*" (Revelation 2:4 NIV).

When I realized after my divorce that this is what I had done, I was devastated. How could I forsake the one who died for me so I might be forgiven? Repentance was the first step back. Then, as the Lord healed my grief and sinful attitudes, he taught me to cling to him and develop an attitude of praise.

Prayer: *Thank you, Dear Lord, for your wonderful plan of salvation. Thank you for not giving up on me, for making yourself known to me. Continue to work in me and through me to be a witness of your marvelous grace. In Jesus's name, Amen.*

Son of God, My Savior

You paid the ransom with your blood to set us free.

You welcomed us with open arms and let us be

adopted as your own joint heirs,

protected from the devil's snares,

sheltered from the world's worst cares.

Praise God, you ransomed me.

How could I not receive your love? You rescued me.

Deception's trap had sucked me in, you salvaged me.

Confusion, loneliness and pride

had tried to drive me from your side.

But in your love I still abide.

By grace, you pardoned me.

Futility would be my lot without your love,

without the constant hope of life with God above.

You turned the light on in my soul.

You cleansed from sin and made me whole.

To love and serve you is my goal. You liberated me!

Judith Vander Wege

Lament and Surprising Mercy

As a representative of the people, the prophet speaks a four -part lament to God: "*Where are your zeal and your might? Your tenderness and compassion are withheld from us*" (Isaiah 63:15).

Have you ever felt like God was far away and did not care about you anymore? Is this God's fault?

People need to take responsibility for their own actions. Or are we puppets on a string, doing what God makes us do? It is true that fallen humans are unable to respond to God without his softening their hearts. But the fact is God has already done everything necessary to reconcile humans with God.

If God loved us enough to die for us, the problems we have in our lives are not his fault. Could it be that we are not trusting him and following his guidance closely enough? God "*acts on behalf of those who wait for him...who gladly do right*" (verse 4-5). Waiting indicates trust in God. Evidence of such trust is a life of godliness.

In Isaiah 64:6-7, we see the contradiction: God helps those

who "*gladly do right,*" yet they cannot do right. God wants fellowship with people, but hc cannot stand sin. What is the solution?

Isaiah repeats the petition, saying we all belong to the God who created us and adopted us. He pleads with God to restore his people to himself.

Chapter 64 seems to be written from the standpoint of the people, who think God has abandoned them. I remember feeling abandoned by God and angry at him.

God answers the lament, because the real issue is continued rebellion. The people say the reason they did not call on God was that he hid from them and let them be destroyed by their sins. Yet God says he was ready to be sought and found by them, but they refused to call on him.

God is merciful for those who do not know him. He keeps drawing them with his love to help them come to him and know him. But those who have known him, who then turn away and stubbornly refuse to follow and obey him, will be judged.

But God is merciful to these rebels, too. Isaiah 65:2 says God has been waiting for his people to return to his open arms, but they will not come. Even those who are obstinate and go their sinful ways of idolatry instead of his perfect way find if they repent and return to the Lord, he is willing to forgive and welcome them back.

As Isaiah draws his book to a close, he predicts that a new age will dawn. Isaiah 65:17- 25 paints a picture of a wonderful place where God's people will no longer suffer. God will create new heavens and a new earth. It will be a happy, peaceful place with no pain, harm or destruction.

People will not be "robbed and plundered, trapped in holes with no one to rescue." By his mercy, God will have rescued all those who believe his word, choose to obey him, and seek his Holy Spirit's help in living a righteous life. If we make that choice, we will be blessed to live with him forever.

However, if we choose not to believe his word and obey God, if we reject and refuse the rescue God's mercy has offered, we will be trapped in sin and its consequences. Since sin cannot be allowed in heaven, we will be separated from God eternally.

Can you hear the loving Father-God's heart weeping?

Rescued by Mercy

God would rather give hope and abundance than to judge and destroy. As a baby is dependent on its mother to receive nourishment, so will we receive God's gifts when we are in a position to receive them. This gives us comfort and encouragement. The choice is up to us. We can choose to worship the one true God and participate in the new heavens and new earth, or we can choose to reject God, refuse to repent, and be destroyed eternally.

God would much rather be merciful, and he gives his enemies chances to repent. I find this comforting. Perhaps the mistakes and sins of my past can somehow be reworked in God's mighty plan so that he can use that evil for good.

The day is coming when the world system will be defeated. Jesus will reign forever in peace. Then we who belong to him will be with him in heaven forever. Hallelujah!

I praise God for showing me his mercy and providing a way for me to be rescued from the trap of sin. I learned that true happiness comes only through accepting what Jesus Christ has done for us, yielding our lives to him in surrender and obedience.

As I began to know the heart of God more intimately, he

guided me in how to live in relationship with him. I have been "Rescued by God's Mercy." The following song is my response to Go

I LOVE YOU, LORD

I love you, Lord. You're mine forever.
You're my Redeemer, King and Friend.
You've paid the price. Your blood has saved me.
You gave me life that will never end.
You'll never leave. You'll hold me tight.
The devil's lost, You have won the fight.
What now my Lord? What shall I do
to let you know how much I love You?

You gave me peace that I can't fathom,
an inner joy in the midst of pain.
I want to be your chosen vessel.
"To live is Christ, and to die is gain."
You'll lead me on o'er land and sea.
To be with You is where I want to be.
I love you, Lord. I'll yield to you.
A yielded life shows that I love You.

Bibliography:

**Albert Barnes, *Barnes Notes: Notes on the Old Testament, Isaiah.* Grand Rapids, MI: Baker Books, 1851,1998.

***Matthew Henry's Commentary on the Whole Bible. USA: Hendrickson Publishers, Inc. 1991

****Halley, Henry H., *Halley's Bible Handbook,* 23rd ed. Grand Rapids, MI: Zondervan Publishing House, 1962.

*Oswalt, John. *THE NIV APPLICATION COMMENTARY: Isaiah.* Grand Rapids: Zondervan*, 2003.*

Judith Vander Wege

About the Author Page

Judith Vander Wege has 300 + credits mostly in Christian periodicals Including: Evangel, Live, Power for Living, Standard, War Cry, Hi-Call, Alive for Young Teens, Vision, Purpose, Grit, The Lutheran, The Quiet Hour, Foursquare World Advance, Wesleyan Woman, Devotions, The Upper Room, Light From the Word, Bread, Keys for Kids, Harpstring, Christian Library Journal. And in Books: Aglow's *Come Celebrate, Christmas Moments, Heaven Sightings, Lutheran Digest , Penned From the Heart* and others.

Judith and her husband, Paul, live in Orange City, Iowa where they attend First Reformed Church. She wrote a Topical Bible Study guide for the church to use one year. She sings in the Sanctuary choir there and has written the narratives for the past two annual "favorites" concerts. The choir has performed two of her musical compositions, and the children's choir two others. She also sings in the Siouxland Women's Chorus.

Judith is a group leader in the community's Coffee Break Bible Study. For recreation she likes to read and sleep and take walks.

The children and grandchildren of Paul and Judith live in WA, TX, CA, MI, ID, and IA. So they don't get to see them often enough.

Contact Judith at her web page: https://judithvanderwege.com,

or email: judith.vw.4hm@gmail.com

Made in the USA
Columbia, SC
03 February 2020

87380523R00083